WILD HORSE HUNTERS

By

Mac (O.H.) McClelland

Preface

He was nervous! He sensed a danger that he could not see or smell. Maybe his inner being sensed the two sets of field glasses that were watching him.

He was a beautiful, well-proportioned animal, unusually so for a wild horse: a blue roan with jet-black mane and tail and a narrow white blaze on his face.

His herd of mares waited restlessly below him at the mouth of a small box canyon. The roan stud was always nervous going into that canyon, but the water was cold and the day had been hot. The fact that a new line of shrubs had suddenly grown up in the vicinity of the mouth of the canyon, did not help alleviate his unease.

A large mare beginning to drift toward the canyon mouth helped him to make up his mind. Rearing up on his back legs, with the setting sun glistened on his glossy hide, he gave a loud snort and dashed down the slope to sweep past his harem and lead them into the canyon for a last drink, before night fell.

The herd broke into a run to follow the blue stallion and in seconds, they all disappeared around a bend with only the cloud of dust remaining to mark their passing.

Two men dashed from their hiding place, downwind from the canyon mouth, and each taking up the end of a twenty-foot aluminium panel, they carried it across the canyon entry. It took three more trips, before the canyon mouth was closed. The panels were of lightweight metal, six foot high, covered with artificial pine branches. When locked together, they made an impenetrable barrier that only the finest jumper could escape. To help defer an attempt, three short poles with silk flags were raised and attached to the fence. The slight breeze kept them fluttering.

The two men stood back to survey their work, moping the sweat off their brows.

"Dang, Red. That was just too easy! I didn't think that blue son-of a gun could be fooled that easy." The taller of the two crowed.

"Well, the hard part is yet to come, pard," the other replied.

"Sure, but you can't ride them till you've caught them. I counted twenty-eight mares and colts. Mister Cooper will be pleased." The taller one responded.

Meeting in Iraq as members of an elite army fighting force, Red Iverson and Parker Williams had formed an unbreakable bond that continued after their separation from the military. Both men had grown up in mid America on a farm/ranch and were stifled by the thought of living in a populated area. Stocky and of medium height, Red Iverson ran the danger of being overweight, should he discontinue his active life. His freckled face sunburned easily. so he frequently applied sun lotion to his face and arms. Red unruly hair escaped from under the battered felt hat; its sweat stains had almost eradicated the original tan color. Faded jeans were stuffed into engineer's boots, which he swapped for high-heeled western boots, when he rode his horse.

An optimist almost to an extreme, and regardless of his red hair, his even temper and natural good humor made instant friends of all he met. His love of outdoor life led him to apply for employment with the Bureau of Land Management (BLM). Upon his acceptance, he was elated to be assigned to the Wyoming department responsible for the horse herds around Adobe Town. His superiors quickly recognized his knowledge and love for horses, and sent him out on the range to observe and report on the teeming herds of wild horses.

Living alone in the wilds was unacceptable, so he was given the task of choosing and hiring an assistant. He quickly e-mailed his friend, Parker Williams from his army days. Parker wasted no time in joining him and the two soon established a permanent camp near a small spring. Life was good!

Using the time honored system for catching wild

horses, Red and Parker had fenced a known water hole, and waited until a wild stallion led his band in to drink, and then slammed the gate shut.

Using modern aluminum portable fencing with an occasional steel post, driven into the ground with a sledgehammer, they could erect a fence in a very short time. The fence is easily camouflaged with artificial tree limbs, and the horses, though suspicious initially, will accept the fence as a natural barrier.

CHAPTER 1

The Hunter's Beginning

Richard M. Cooper, the Second, was the Rawlins Field Director of the Wyoming BLM.

He did not liked to be called Dick, and Red Iverson was the only one that got away with calling him 'Boss'.

Red faced him across the desk, pacing as he talked.

"Boss, I can make small drives and hand pick the really good studs and mares to turn back into the wild. Eventually, we will have first class horses ranging out there. People will be crowding to adopt a wild horse, instead of just attracting the horse lovers that don't want those broomtails put down. There are some great stallions out there, if we could only pair them up with a harem of good mares. Give me the Adobe herds for a couple of years. I know I can produce."

Richard M. Cooper leaned back in his chair.

"All right, Red. Send me a list of what you need, and the approximate costs. Also, send me your plan of attack, and I will try to sell it to the big brass. That is all I can promise you."

Later, Red and Parker huddled over coffee and pie at Ma's Kitchen. Red had his iPad on the table and was making a list of supplies that were needed.

"We need about three miles of that aluminum

fencing," Parker offered.

"Our little quads with their trailers are fine, but we need a big four wheel drive pick-up and a stock trailer. And don't forget the camouflage tree limbs," Red added.

The two wranglers pored over their list and Red, using his iPad, looked up prices, and Parker totaled the figures.

"Wow," Red exclaimed and Parker whistled, as they arrived at a total expense!

Back in Richard Cooper's office, Red handed the supply list across the desk to his boss, who scanned it without comment.

"How do you plan to operate, Red?" Cooper's face showed no indication of his feelings.

"I have a good sized box canyon picked out with good water and grazing," Red began. It's called, Raidy's Springs. A grand blue roan stallion uses it part of the time. I hope to trap him and use the canyon as the base. I will haul the inferior mares into town and fence three or four more water holes to trap other herds. I plan to transport the best mares back to the blue roan until he has a full herd and then turn him out. I figure I will have close to one hundred culls by then. Hopefully I will find another good stud and repeat the procedure."

"Looks good on paper," his superior grunted. "We need to thin those herds by fifteen hundred head. How long will that take?"

Red ran a hand through his unruly hair. "Gee, Boss, a year or so, I reckon. Don't know how it will work in the winter, if we get some snow. I could use hay to coax the horses into my traps. They are apt to eat snow and ignore the water holes!"

Richard Cooper pushed the supply list back to Red.

"Add fifty ton of alfalfa. You don't have anything in there for your own supplies," he remarked. "Put in ten dollars per day for that and add ten thousand for hiring extra help. You need an extra ten thousand for miscellaneous. Total that all up," he directed.

Looking slightly dazed, Red accepted the list, he, and Parker spent several minutes following their instructions

—

before returning it.

"Well, it is still well below the cost of our last big drive! Those helicopters were expensive!" Cooper allowed a faint smile of satisfaction cross his face. "Maybe I can sell it. Improving the quality of the herds should be worth something, too."

Richard Cooper stood up, indicating that the meeting was over. "I should know within a week. I will call you."

In spite of Parker's words of caution, Red was sure it was a "done deal" and immediately commenced a search for a good used four-wheeled drive pick-up and stock trailer. He particularly wanted a used stock trailer, as some modifications would be needed to adapt it to their needs.

He was elated to find both in a three-year-old truck with low mileage and a matching fifth wheel trailer at half the price of new ones. The seller was also an accomplished welder and agreed to the building on of some pipe racks to carry the metal fencing.

It was an anti-climax for Red , when his boss called with the good news. He had the money that he needed, and the go-ahead to execute his plan. He immediately called the owner of the truck and trailer. He also ordered two miles of the fencing. He and Parker were in the business of trapping wild horses!

CHAPTER 2

First Catch

Parker stopped driving the iron post into the ground to mop the sweat from his eyes. Nearby, Red finished assembling another twenty-foot panel.

"Only three more posts, Parker. I could finish them while you start putting on the camouflage tree limbs," Red offered.

"Naw! You are better at making those branches look real," Parker replied as they carried the last panel in place and secured it. "I'll finish the posts."

A couple hours later, the two men stood back to admire their handiwork.

"Pretty nifty," Parker exclaimed. "Sure beats the old way of building fences. Now, if we can just coax the blue stud to bring his herd in to drink."

An apparent line of evergreen shrubs had sprung up across the canyon mouth. Four panels had been removed from the center to allow entrance and stored close by. They would be carried back in place after the horses entered the trap.

"What do you think about our taking the Quads out and kinda moseying the herd over this way," Parker inquired.

"Be too late today, by the time we get the truck back to camp," Red responded. "Maybe about noon tomorrow."

The blue roan stallion ceased grazing to watch with

interest, as two small vehicles appeared. Their heavily muffled engines were just barely discernible. The two quads spread out as they neared, but stopped before they approached so close as to make the horses run.

The stallion went briefly back to grazing, but the proximity of the vehicles made him a little testy, so he rounded up his mares and moved them another half mile away before resuming cropping grass. After about twenty minutes, the quads moved closer and stopped again. Again, the blue roan moved his herd away from them. This was repeated several times until Raidy's Springs came in sight and then, just as quietly as they appeared, the two vehicles dropped out of sight.

Keeping to the low ground to escape detection from the wild stallion, the two wranglers drove on to Raidy's Springs and a mile past it. They carefully hid their machines downwind and returned to the canyon trap on foot, hiding in a previously prepared location. Here they laid back to wait patiently, hoping the stallion would lead his mares to the Springs this afternoon.

Parker took advantage of the situation, placed his hat over his eyes, and went to sleep. Red was way too excited to sleep. This was his first try at trapping wild horses and his usual optimist nature was suffering a relapse! He was suddenly afraid the blue roan stallion would be too clever to walk into the canyon!

Lord, I ask Your help on this thing. I think this job is a good thing, and if it is, I ask You to send that blue roan and his herd into our corral. However it works, though, Lord, I thank You!"

He could see a remnant of the herd with his field glasses and his eyes were glued to them as they wandered to and fro, searching for choice morsels. After what seemed like hours, he detected a positive movement in the herd. They were headed this way at a fast walk.

Red punched his sleeping partner in the ribs.

"Wake up, Parker. That blue son of a gun is coming this way!"

After some hesitation, the blue roan stallion led his

band into the trap and on to water. The two wranglers hurriedly closed the opening with the waiting panels.

Giving each other a high five, they stood back and mopped their sweaty faces.

"Dang, Red. That was just too easy! I didn't think that blue stallion could be fooled that easy," Parker crowed.

"Well, the hard part is yet to come, pard," the other replied.

"Sure, but you can't ride them til you've caught them. I counted twenty-eight mares and a half dozen colts. Mister Cooper will be pleased," Parker chuckled.

"Parker, I saw four or five of those mares that are going to be kept with the roan, plus a couple of colts."

"Aw, Red, I know you. You would keep and feed every one of those little worthless broomtails," Parker retorted.

"You're right, Parker. I hate killing of any kind. Reckon I got to see too much of it in the army. It was bad enough in the Great Sand box! Lucky I wasn't in Vietnam or Korea," Red said.

"Well, we will let Blue and his harem get used to their new home and built a couple more traps. There is that gray stud that ranges near Willow Creek. We will start there tomorrow," Red went on. "Then we can come back and put together a small corral and loading ramp. Thank You, Lord for Your speedy answer to my prayer!"

Willow Creek was entirely different from Raidy's Springs in that there were almost no natural barriers. The entire area must be fenced. Willow Creek started with a series of springs, joining forces to become a year round creek and was a favorite with the wild horses, because of the succulent grass that grew along the stream.

The big four-wheeled drive truck arrived early, as the sun was just peeking over the hills to the east. The stock trailer that it pulled was stacked high with unassembled fence panels.

"Parker, I been rethinking our stratagem, while you were driving out. I think we should just put up fencing today and tomorrow on the back side of the trap, decorate it with pine limbs and let it sit for a couple days. Maybe the mustangs will get used to some fencing without catching on that it is a trap," Red explained. "What do you think?"

"That's good thinking, Red. We got a quarter mile of fencing with us. That should go across the back and up each side a little way. Let's see how those broomies react." Parker stretched and began unloading the aluminum fencing.

About mid-morning, both of the men headed back to the truck for water.

"Red, we haven't talked much about your plan for loading up the culls to take into Rawlings. What is your idea?" Parker squatted on his heels and laid off his hat.

"Well, as you know; it is just an idea. I haven't ever tried it yet," Red responded. "I intend to build a small corral in the entry with just two panel wide entry, and put a loading chute off to one side, leading to the stock trailer. Hopefully, by using our two geldings, we can drive the band into the small corral where we can cut out the blue roan and the better mares and colts and release them back into the large pen. Loading the culls into the trailer will take some doing, but I think we can do it."

"Wow! I hadn't ever thought it through." Parker scratched his head and then replaced his hat. "You ought to think about that Indian that wanted to hire on with us. What was his name? Walter Wiley? He had a great cutting horse and seemed like an eager worker. Plus, we need to know where the herds are watering. He would handle that okay."

"You are right, Parker. I'll call the boss and have him send him out if he can find him," Red responded. "A third rider could be a life saver. I got to get used to having the money to spend! Well, let's get this fence built and I will call, when we get back to camp."

"Red, I have that Indian's cell number in my phone, if you want to try it." Parker tossed in , as he headed back to the fence line.

The two wranglers worked steadily with a short break at noon for lunch. About three o'clock, Red called a halt.

"Parker, we need to be out of here, before any horse herd comes in for water," Red explained. "Let's cover the rest of the fence with branches and quit for the day."

As they finished packing up their tools, Parker had a suggestion.

"Why don't we swing by Raidy's Springs and see how the blue roan and his harem are doing? Good time to check on the road to there, if we are going to haul some mares back and forth!"

"Good thinking! Let's do it," Red responded. "Go ahead, you're driving."

About halfway to the Springs, they had to cross a small gully. They made it across with the empty stock trailer but they would not be able to cross with it full of horses.

"That aluminum bridging will come in handy here." Red smiled. "I'm glad we included some on our supply list."

The wild horses heard their truck before they arrived, and stampeded to the far end of the pasture and out of sight.

"I don't believe they like us," Parker laughed as he dismounted from the truck.

"No and they aren't't going to get any tamer, locked up here," Red said seriously. "I am rethinking my plan a bit. How about we get this loading chute built here next and get those culls into town. The longer they stay here, the more grass they will eat."

"No reason to hold off that I can think of," Parker agreed. "You want to start a list of material, now?"

Parker pulled out a clipboard from the cab as Red began to step off the distances for the new corral and loading chute, calling out each panel and post.

Walt was a welcome sight, as he was waiting in camp for them when they arrived. He rode a stocky painted mustang, a favorite among the Indians.

Having loaded up the trailer the night before, the three wranglers got an early start the next day. By nightfall, the corral was completed, except for the mobile loading ramp. They opened the four panel entrance and pulled two of them out to help direct the horses into the corral.

"Good job, guys! Tomorrow is the big day!" Red grinned his satisfaction. "I need to be loaded up by noon to get the culls to town before dark. Can we do it?"

"I think so," Walt offered. "Three good riders on

three good horses!"

That drew a chuckle from the other two.

The sun was still hidden behind the Wyoming hills, when the big pick-up, pulling the stock trailer, pulled up to the new corral. The men lost no time unloading the three saddled horses from the trailer and parking the rig back away from the corral. The wild horses were more afraid of the truck and trailer than the corral fences.

All the wild horses that were in sight had fled at their approach, but the three wranglers rode slowly to the far end of the pasture, circling behind the herd. Again, holding their mounts to a walk, they spread out, commencing to drive the herd before them.

A loud blast originated from the big stallion as he wheeled back and forth, driving the mares toward the apparently open entrance. The wranglers spurred their horses to keep up, as it became apparent that the stallion was doing all the work for them! With luck, all they needed to do was get the gate panels in place, before the wild horses found out, they were cornered and broke back out of the corral.

It was over within minutes! The riders jumped from their horses and had the panels in place before the dust settled. The herd was in the corral! The three men looked at each other in amazement. The sun broke over the hills to flood the scene with light.

"Wow! Can you believe that," cried the vociferous Parker. "Maybe that blue son-of-a-gun will load them in the trailer for us."

"I think the Great Spirit was helping us," the Indian laughed.

"Well, I'm grateful to one and all," Red agreed. "Walt, let's see, how good your paint horse is in cutting out. My idea is to put Parker on the gate and you and I cut the stud out and back into the pasture, plus four or five of the best mares and yearling colts. Let's do it!"

Three yearling colts had caught Red's eye and were obvious offspring of the blue roan stallion. They proved to be on the outside of the bunched mares and were quickly cut out and chased back out the gate. Next, the stallion, upon seeing the colts seemingly free, wanted to join them and was obliged, as he dashed back through the entrance.

Reluctant to leave his harem, the blue roan whistled loudly from the outside, helping to break up the bunched mares and one by one, Red and Walt eased the mares, which Red had chosen, out of the herd and out of the corral.

Only an hour had elapsed, but the saddle horses were tiring. Red changed places with Parker.

"Parker, you and Walt try to thin them a bit and drive them by me. I think there is one more mare, a mouse color, that I want to keep," Red directed.

"I have her, Boss," Walt called out from back in the herd. "Open the gate!"

Walt rushed out of the herd, pushing a good looking mouse colored mare. She dodged through the narrow opening and was free! The blue stallion, seemingly satisfied with his reduced herd, quickly led them away.

"Parker, bring up the truck and unhook the loading ramp. Walt, help him roll it into place. Let's get those culls loaded," Red called out.

As Parker was backing the stock trailer into position against the loading ramp, Walt called to Red.

"Boss, I might can lead this bunch into the trailer with my paint horse. Can I try it?"

"Go for it, Walt. Whatever works," Red replied.

Walt led his saddle horse to the bottom of the loading ramp and left him there, while he went on into the trailer. When Red and Parker had crowded the herd to that end of the corral, Walt whistled to his horse, who immediately walked up the ramp and into the trailer. Several of the wild ones followed him, and Red and Parker pushed the others smoothly up the ramp and into the trailer!

Working his way carefully through the crowded trailer, Walt rode his paint horse to the back and down the ramp. He grinned widely, as he dismounted beside Red.

Red shook his head and grinned back at him before checking his watch.

"I can't believe it. We are all loaded up and it isn't even ten o'clock yet," he burst out. "If our luck holds out, I might get back to camp tonight! I need to call the boss and tell him I'm coming."

"What do you want us to do while you're gone, Red," Parker inquired.

"Load the cooler on my black horse." Red indicated his saddle horse. "And ride on back to Willow Creek and work on the fence until one o'clock, then ride out to see what wild horses are in the vicinity, who might use the Creek. Hopefully, I'll see you back in camp about sundown."

Red climbed into the cab, as the others mounted their horses and rode away.

The dirt road was in reasonable shape, and the fifth wheel stock trailer with its double tandem wheels was heavily loaded, but the big Chevy, pulling with all four wheels with large desert tires, moved steadily along at fifteen to twenty miles per hour.

CHAPTER 3

A Lady Visitor

Richard Cooper, Red's boss was in a jovial mood, as he gazed across his desk to the dust covered Red Iverson.

"That's great! Two dozen brought in on your first try," he exulted. "I question your turning those yearlings back, though. They will be inbred and defeat your idea of improving the herds."

"Not so, Boss. I intend to move them to the next good stallion, that I trap, and move his yearlings to the blue roan. I hope to move the good yearlings every couple years, after this, if you will let me," Red defended himself.

"Sounds like you have it well thought out," Mister Cooper acknowledged. "When do you expect to bring in your next load?"

"I can't predict how soon that a herd will water there, but we will have Willow Springs fenced in a couple of days," Red replied. "With Walt helping, we can post a guard at a couple water holes at a time to close the gates. The Seeps will be our next trap."

Richard Cooper started to rise, and then dropped back into his chair.

"Almost forgot! There is a young lady, a commercial photographer, over at the hotel. Her name is Teresa Castell. We have been instructed to show her every courtesy, and your job is to take her out to your camp and show her the

---

various wild horse bands for her to photograph."

"Aw, Boss! I don't have time to escort some dame around, taking pictures. I need to--," Red started to complain, but was cut short by Richard Cooper.

"This isn't up for debate, Iverson. The Bureau is under fire from horse lovers all over, who don't believe there is a need to control the numbers of wild horses," he announced. "It is important to the Bureau, and you that she gets access to whatever she wishes, and gives a good report on our and your activities!"

"But, Boss, we don't have any facilities for women visitors at the camp," Red protested.

Richard Cooper stood up. The interview was over!

"Take my vehicle to the hotel and meet her," he directed. "Find out what she expects. You can leave my car at the corrals or wherever. Let me know."

Red walked up to the desk of Rawlings' finest hotel.

"I am looking for Teresa Castell. Could you help me," he asked the clerk.

The clerk looked at Red's unkempt condition with disdain.

"I believe that is Miss Castell over there." He pointed to a figure, occupying an armchair, across the lobby.

All of a sudden, aware of his dusty attire, Red flushed with embarrassment, as he crossed the lobby to confront the lady.

"Good afternoon, Ma'am. I'm Red Iverson. Mister Cooper sent me over," he stated.

The lady put down the newspaper, which she had been studying.

"It is Miss, not Ma'am," she replied coolly, and then a grin spread over her face. "You look like you have been dragged through the corral!"

Red grinned back at her, recovering his good humor.

"You could say that literally. Plus a long dusty road," he replied.

Teresa Castell stood up and offered her hand. In her western boots, she was almost as tall as Red. Dressed in blue jeans and yellow western shirt, she was an attractive woman.

18

A gray Stetson hat, covering her short dark brown hair, completed her ensemble.

"Thank you for seeing me. Would you call me, Teresa," she asked. "I understand you have just brought in a load of wild horses."

"Yes, Teresa, I did. Would you like to see them," Red responded, accepting her hand. "I have the boss's car outside."

"That would be super, Red," Teresa enthused. "I have my camera and gear. Could we go now?"

"Sure could. Can I carry something?"

They stepped out of Mister Cooper's SUV next to a corral full of milling horses.

"That's my rig," Red pointed to his truck and trailer, parked near-by. "Do you know horses, Teresa?"

"As a matter of fact, I do. My father raised quarter horses, and he also liked to trade horses. I learned very young to ride and care for horses," Teresa replied as she approached the corral and leaned against the fence, inspecting the wild mares. "Not very impressive lot," she added.

Red nodded, but said nothing.

Teresa climbed part way up the rail fence and snapped several pictures with her camera.

"What happens to them now," she inquired, a bit coolly.

"I don't have anything to do with them after this point, but I understand they are shipped to the Circle Y Ranch, over in the Wind River area," Red replied.

"And from there to the glue factory," Teresa added. She made no effort to hide her bitterness.

Red stared at her. Shocked!

"Oh no, Teresa! None of them are killed! They halter break them, and tame them somewhat, and offer them to the public for adoption. Where did you get that idea?" Red was half angry.

A little uncertain now, Teresa was unprepared for Red's vehemence!

"I was told that some of the States are ignoring the

19

law against destroying the horses because of the cost to feed them," Teresa responded. "I don't see, why they can't just leave them alone in the wild, like God intended for them!"

"I assume that the one that gave you that information was an authority and could substantiate their accusation," Red retorted.

"Well, no. I never saw any proof," Teresa admitted.

"Should you ever find that Wyoming is guilty of that, I will quit my job," Red declared.

"But why can't the horses be left alone to live as they wish," Teresa persisted. "Why must the government interfere?"

"Mister Cooper indicated that you wanted to come out to my camp." Red seemingly left the subject.

"Yes, I would. I have a Jeep Wrangler that will go almost anywhere," Teresa answered. "Could I just follow you out?"

"Sure, but I kick up an awful dust cloud. If you have GPS, you can dial in the location of my camp, and I will follow you. We should leave pronto to get there before sundown," Red informed her. "I think I can show you, why the wild horse program is necessary."

"I am checked out. Drop me off at the hotel and we are ready to roll," Teresa responded.

The sun was still an hour away from sunset when Teresa stopped her Wrangler and climbed from the vehicle. Red parked his rig next to her.

"On my! Is this it?" She looked around with dismay written across her face. "Where is the bathroom?"

"It's, ah, behind those two shrubs," Red pointed. "The toilet paper is in that gallon can. You'll see it."

"We aren't set up for coed occupation. I tried to tell Mister Cooper," Red remarked, when Teresa returned.

He was surprised to hear Teresa chuckling

"That's an understatement," she responded. "I suppose you take a bath out of your canteens."

"Oh, nothing that crude!" Red was now chuckling also. "We generally use that flat stone in the creek." Pointing again. "We can erect a blanket to give you privacy.

The water is not too chilly, especially after a warm day."

They were interrupted by the arrival of Parker and Walt, leading Red's saddle horse. Red and the girl walked over to greet them.

"Red takes a load of broomtail horses to town and comes back with you. I'd say he made a pretty good trade," was Parker's response to the introduction. "Can I take the next load in, Boss?"

"Better take off a couple layers of this desert dust before you try your hand at trading," Teresa laughed.

"The boss isn't exactly Mister Clean, and he did okay," Walt chimed in.

"Enough of this," Red interrupted. "Parker, it's your night to cook, so you get to clean up first. You and Walt throw up a couple of blankets around our bath site and wash up. I'll unsaddle and take care of our horses."

"Could I help you, Red? I'm good around horses," Teresa asked. "I would like to help anywhere that I can, so as not to be a burden."

"Sure. Grab Walt's paint and follow me."

When Teresa and Red returned from taking care of the saddle horses, Parker was busy in one of the tents.

"We have one tent just for the kitchen," Red remarked. "It is pretty tight to keep the varmints out. It is as modern as I could find with a bottle gas refrigerator, freezer, stove and oven. We use LED lighting, but have some propane lanterns for back up. Mister Cooper gave us a generous food allowance, so we eat as good as we can cook."

"Do you all sleep in the other tent," Teresa inquired.

"Only if it is cold or rainy. We all have air mattresses and prefer sleeping under the stars. You are welcome to use the tent while you're here," Red answered. "Just prepare for company, if a thunderstorm blows up."

Shortly, they sat down to a supper of fried pork chops, hot baked beans and potato salad. There was a choice of white bread or whole wheat with several jellies. Canned peaches was dessert, and hot coffee was used to wash it all down.

"Oh my! This is first class and I'm starved," Teresa said between mouthfuls, while Parker beamed.

"My turn to cook tomorrow night," Walt expounded. "If the boss will give me a little time, I make soda biscuits that melt in your mouth!"

"If my vote counts, I am for giving you the required time," Teresa laughed.

Teresa insisted on helping clean up, while Walt built a small mesquite fire. It was a moonless night and the stars dominated the sky. Red pulled out camp chairs and Walt lit a cigarette and Parker a pipe.

"What do you have planned for tomorrow," Teresa asked.

"Boss, Walt and I can finish at Willow Creek tomorrow. There were horse tracks around our fence. We saw three separate herds within a couple miles of there," Parker stated.

"Good! We will try that same trick of herding one of the stallions with his harem toward the Creek day after tomorrow," Red rubbed his hands in satisfaction. "I will take one of the quads tomorrow and show Teresa the blue roan and inspect some of the grazing grounds. Maybe get some photos of some other wild herds. Don't forget to build us a blind to hide in. Use your best guess, as to what is down wind."

"I don't want to be a bother," Teresa began to protest, but Red held his hand.

"Mister Cooper made it clear to me that getting you first-hand knowledge of the horse herds was my priority," he cut her short. "Besides," with a grin, "I expect to enjoy my job!"

The next morning, Parker and Walt loaded the truck and trailer with fence panelling and left for Willow Creek. Red and Teresa boarded one of the quads and headed for Raidy's Springs.

"This quad is so quiet," Teresa exclaimed. "Why is that?"

"I wanted to get around without frightening the wild horses, so I had them double muffled and wrapped every noisy joint that we could," Red replied. "If I drive carefully, we can get fairly close to the herd without spooking them."

By keeping some high ground between them and Raidy's Springs, Red was able to drive near the corral without detection. They left the quad and crept around some shrubbery to give Teresa a look at the blue stallion and the few mares that he had left. Red handed Teresa his field glasses.

"He's beautiful," Teresa exclaimed, "and those colts are built just like him. What are you going to do with them?"

As she spoke, Teresa was digging out her camera and snapping a few pictures of the horses and surroundings.

"I hope to trap more good mares to add to his herd before I turn him back out," Red replied. The yearling colts I will hold and give them to the next good stallion that I catch."

"Oh, so you aren't just thinning the herds, you are trying to upgrade the ones that you leave. Why isn't the Bureau advertising that," Teresa inquired.

"I just got started on the program," Red confessed. "This was our first attempt. Parker and Walt are finishing our second corral. There is a gray stallion with several good mares that I am hoping to catch in that one, maybe in the next few evenings."

They got back into the quad, and Red drove on out in the open meadow area and stopped. Teresa looked at him inquiringly.

"I want you to look at the grass here," Red explained. "What do you see?"

"It is pretty short. This area has been heavily grazed off," Teresa replied.

"I am going to head on over toward the Seeps. I want you to stop me periodically and examine the grass," Red requested as he drove off.

Several stops later, Teresa had photographed several locations of the grass. Teresa threw up her hands.

"The whole area that we have driven over has been heavily grazed," she admitted.

"Yes, and this is July. Except for some scattered thunderstorms, we won't get much more rainfall. What are the horses going to live on this winter?" Red looked distressed. "There is a plateau up ahead, where you can see a

---

goodly distance. I think you will be able to get a better idea of the number of wild horse herds that we are dealing with."

An hour later, Red turned off the main trail and started up a winding, steep trail.

"I'll go as far as I can, but we will have to hoof it the last quarter mile," Red remarked, as he bumped over a rocky outcrop. "The view is worth it!"

Ahead was a rockslide that completely obliterated the trail. Red stopped the quad, and backed it around the way they had come.

"Grab a bottle of water, Teresa. It's a good climb, but short," Red reported, as he exited the quad.

Red led the way up the slope. Beside the bottle of water in his belt, he carried a round cylinder about three feet long. About thirty minutes later, they topped the last hump and came out on the level. Teresa dropped to the ground with a groan.

"Is this any way to treat a guest," she whimpered.

Red chuckled. "You just had too much city life. Take a few minutes, then get up and look around. It is worth the struggle!"

"Oh, my!" Teresa struggled to a sitting position. The horizon stretched thirty to forty miles away in two directions.

Red opened the cylinder to reveal a large telescope with folded tripod.

"I like to use this, when I need some distance," he remarked as he set it up. "Here take a look."

"Oh, my," Teresa said again. "I see dozens of herds of horses. Are you going to catch all of them?"

Red shrugged. "I can only take one step at a time. Let me take a look."

"Here you can see Willow Creek and my hard working crew." Red turned the telescope back the way that they had come and relinquished his place to Teresa.

"I see them! The pen is almost finished," Teresa cried.

"Sweep the area nearby. See if you can spot that gray stallion and his band," Red encouraged.

Several minutes lapsed as Teresa peered through the

telescope. Suddenly she froze.

"I think I found them. Oh, he is huge! Almost like a Clydesdale, and gray as ashes! The mares are really good ones, too. I think he is a fighter. Look!" Teresa eased away from the telescope. Being careful not to move it.

"That's him," Red was peering through the telescope now. "I don't really want to keep him, but I want his mares for the blue roan."

Red pulled a map from his pocket and noted the location of the herd on it.

"We will try to ease them over to Willow Creek tomorrow. The Seeps will be our next trap. Give me a minute. I'll see if I can locate it." Red continued his search on the telescope.

"Here it is. Several wild horses near there. Want a look?" Red backed away to let Teresa see.

Tired, dusty and dirty, Red and Teresa arrived at the base camp to discover that Parker and Walt had already arrived. Walt had mixed his biscuits and was anxiously awaiting their arrival.

After supper, they retired around the mesquite campfire and exchanged experiences for the day.

"Those biscuits and sausage gravy were a real treat," Teresa complimented Walt.

Walt grinned his pleasure.

"We put up two blinds, Boss. One on each side of the gate so we can pick which one is the best," Parker explained.

"We saw that big gray stallion, not far from the Creek," Red revealed. "We will take a load of fencing over to the Seeps and work until noon and then take the quads and try to work the big gray and his harem over toward Willow Creek like we did with the blue roan. It worked once. Maybe it will twice!"

As the fire dimmed, so did the eyelids.

"I'm pooped," Teresa admitted. "Will you all excuse me?"

"It's that time," Parker chimed in. "Me for the sack."

All rose to their feet and headed for their beds.

—

CHAPTER 4

The Big Stallion

It was shortly after noon, and the two quads were headed back to Willow Creek to locate the gray stallion and his band. Red and Teresa were in one vehicle, while Parker and Walt rode the other. They had split up to cover more area and keep in contact via hand held radios.

Walt was the first to spot the band and Parker, who was driving, cut back to circle around behind the horses. Red soon made his appearance and they spread out, with several hundred yards between them, to begin their game.

The plains were wide open and there was no place to hide so the two quads just slowly advanced on the grazing horse herd. The big gray stallion had spotted them immediately, and stopped his grazing to watch them, as they slowly approached.

At some point, his curiosity turned to apprehension and he began to step around nervously. The quads continued to advance slowly to a point, where the stallion finally decided that they were getting too close to his harem. He trotted over to his band, and began to drive them ahead of him before running by them, and leading them a quarter mile to a safer location to graze.

At Red's signal, the two quads again began a slow advance on the horse herd. The scenario was repeated three times and Red had decided that one more advance would be as close to Willow Creek, as they would go.

On the fourth advance of the quads, the stallion's demeanor changed. Instead of driving the mares away, he faced the quads and began to walk slowly toward them as they advanced. Red's quad was the closest and was chosen by the gray stallion as the subject of his investigation.

When the stallion was about three hundred yards away, Red started to get nervous and turned to Teresa.

"You know, I think that big boy is tired of us harassing him and is going to return the favor," he remarked.

The gray stallion broke into a trot now, his ears laid back and mouth open! Red put the quad in gear and sped off the opposite direction, desperate to put some distance between him and the irate stallion! There was no question now, the stallion was at full speed, intent on attacking the offending vehicle!

The rough terrain prevented Red from going too fast, while trying to miss the larger of the potholes.

"Red, he is gaining on us," Teresa cried franticly, her eyes were glued to the approaching animal!

"Teresa, there is a wire loop next to my right foot," Red replied as he dodged around a steep wash. "Pull up on it!"

As Teresa complied, the smooth quiet throb of the quad engine suddenly changed to a full-throated roar! The noise was deafening! The stallion slowed immediately to a trot, his eyes wide and ears pointed forward with fear. He spun around to gallop back to his harem!

"Whooey! That angry stud was going to stomp us into the ground," Red exclaimed as he pulled the quad to a stop and shut down the noisy engine.

"What happened," Teresa half shouted, her face white. "What did I do?"

"That wire you pulled opens a by-pass to the mufflers," Red answered. "We have a straight pipe from the engine. I use it this way, when I am driving cattle or horses."

Parker drove alongside them. "Hey, that was one teed off animal! Are you guys okay?"

Teresa assured him that she was fine

———

"I think that gray devil forgot to read the script," she chuckled, "about, who is supposed to chase who!"

"You are lucky that wasn't the blue roan that was chasing you," Walt chimed in. "He can move twice as fast as that gray!"

"Boss, I think we need to start carrying our pistols, again," Parker exclaimed. "If you had hit a bad wash and stalled, you would have been a goner!"

"You're right, Parker, starting tonight. Well, he has to water the mares somewhere tonight," Red got back to business. "You two go back to camp and grab some grub and take a roundabout way to Willow Creek. You hide out until midnight. If the horses haven't watered there yet, I will relieve you then. I'll cruise around with this noise-maker to keep his attention, until you are out of sight. Then we will go back to camp. I'll try to catch some shuteye, so I can stay awake tonight."

In spite of his objections, Teresa had insisted on accompanying Red on his vigil. They had relieved Parker and Walt at midnight, as planned. The moon had risen late and supplied a modicum of light. They had chatted in whispers the first hour, and then fell silent, each with their own thoughts.

The night was cool and Red had provided a heavy blanket for them to sit on, keeping them off the damp ground. Suddenly, without comment, Teresa slid over next to Red, placing her arm around his waist. Red looked down at her face and clasping her to him, he gave her a long kiss.

"Been wanting to do that for a long time," he whispered.

"I was beginning to wonder, what was the matter with me," Teresa grinned mischievously. "You can make up for lost--."

"Ssh! Listen!" Red went rigid with attention.

In the distance, they heard a snort, and then shortly a second one.

"Horses out there," Red whispered unnecessarily and rose to his feet quietly.

They peered through the artificial foliage to see a

dark mass moving their way. It continued to advance until only a hundred yards away before stopping. They could make out the larger pale shape, which would be the gray stallion. He stamped his feet, not completely happy, but very thirsty, by this time. After checking the air for strange scents, he finally trotted on through the opening in the fence and headed for the Creek.

When the last horse had gone from sight, Red, accompanied by Teresa, glided from their hideout to the loose fence panels. Carefully, they picked up a panel and carrying it into place, Red fastened the clips. They must get them in place without the stallion hearing them.

Working quietly but quickly, the second panel went up, then the third. On the last panel, however, Teresa tripped as she got near the fence and the metal panel that she was carrying struck the existing one with a loud clang!

"Get on the outside of the fence," Red shouted as he clipped his end to the fence and dashed to her end.

The hoof beats of the running horses were growing louder as he clipped the last panel into place!

"Run for the blind! They might break through!" Red screamed as he backed away from the fence and drew his pistol.

The herd was getting close now and running hard when Red commenced to fire his gun into the air. It seemed that even the gunfire would not deter them, but at his fourth shot, the big stallion veered and ran down the fence line, the mares following!

"Whew! That was close." Red mopped his brow and began to reload his gun.

"Red, you would have been killed, if they hadn't stopped and turned!" Teresa gave his arm a shake.

"I thought the noise of that big Forty-Five would stop them, but I was beginning to doubt. I was afraid they couldn't see the fence in the dark," Red replied with a shake of his head. "Let's get out of here and hope they will settle down. I'll be glad when that big gray is locked up in town!"

The next day was taken up with the three wranglers building a replica of the Raidy's Springs corral and loading pen at Willow Creek. Teresa took her jeep and drove out to photograph as many horse herd as she could.

Unlike the blue roan stallion who had kept as much distance from the workers as he could, the big gray seemed interested in their activities and frequently prowled the fence between them. Obviously in an angry mood, he snorted often and carried his ears back the entire time.

"We best bring that "bad boy halter" with us tomorrow and rig the winch on the truck," Red remarked while they were taking a break for lunch. "That stud is going to give us big trouble and I suspect we will end up dragging him into the trailer. He doesn't seem afraid of us. I think he has been born on a ranch and somehow escaped."

"I think you are right, Boss," Walt agreed. "If he has been rope broke, that could work for us, as I don't think he will drive up the loading ramp."

"Yeah! We need to have a tight saddle cinch and our ropes ready, when we get in the corral with this character," Parker chimed in. "And you know, Red, some heavy praying wouldn't hurt either."

"You're right, Parker," Red replied. "We need to get back to that, we been kinda lax about the Lord, lately."

With all three men working, the corral went up quickly and late afternoon found them back in camp. It was noteworthy that each took the time to examine their saddle girths closely. None of them was looking forward to tackling the big gray stallion.

Teresa drove in just before sundown and was bubbling about the pictures, which she had taken of the wild horses.

"I got a couple of shots of a good looking bay stallion with many nice bay mares. The colts were pretty mangy though, probably inbred. I thought maybe the mares were all the stallion's offspring and separating them would be a good thing," she enthused.

They spent an hour looking at her digital pictures after supper and it was a while before she noticed that the men were quieter than usual.

"What's going on with you guys? Has something happened," she inquired.

"I think we are all wondering if our life insurance premiums are paid up, before tackling that gray monster tomorrow," Parker chuckled.

Teresa noticed an odd looking rope halter laying nearby.

"What is this for," she inquired.

"If you have to lead a horse that hasn't been broke to lead, you are apt to just choke him down, without moving him," Red explained. "This goes over his ears and this braided part goes in his mouth, like a bridle bit, but this loops over and squeezes his nose instead of cutting off his air around his neck. The horse's nose is very sensitive and he learns to lead very quickly!"

"Oh! That seems mean! It must hurt a lot," Teresa protested.

"It only hurts him, if he fights," Red argued. "Horses are smart and they figure it out. Besides, you have to realize that man only weighs a couple hundred pounds, and this big stud weighs over a ton! We need something to level the playing field."

"Wait until you see him in action tomorrow," Walt added his two-cents worth.

"It's breakfast by candle light. I want to be driving horses by dawn," Red closed down the conversation, receiving a collective groan from the others. "I don't want to be unloading horses in town with a flashlight, either," he added, squashing any complaints. "Don't forget to say a prayer. We are definitely going to need His help tomorrow!"

Some of the horses were still sleeping when the three horsemen spread out and started walking them toward the opening in the corral fence, which led to the loading chute. A loud snort alerted them that the big stallion was awake and alert. The wild horses gave little trouble as the trotted across the enclosure and ran through the opening. Quickly, the riders leaped from their mounts and closed the panels to hold them.

"We will try to cut out those good mares and turn them back out," Red directed. If the stud interferes, we will have to rope him and drag him aboard. Walt, you do the

---

31

cutting out."

They had four mares cut out and returned to the larger pen, before the stud took umbrage and attacked! He charged Walt's paint horse, who nimbly evaded the stallion's rush! At Walt's yell, Parker, who was manning the gate, quickly locked the panel and jumped on his waiting horse.

As the stallion turned for another rush at Walt, Red dropped a noose over the stallion's head. Seconds later, Parker also added his lasso, topping Red's. This diverted the stud's attention to Red's black, and his lunge at the black brought Parkers sorrel to its knees.

The stallion screamed in rage, rearing high into the air to strike at the vulnerable black.

"Look out, Red," Teresa screamed from the top of the corral fence!

Walt took advantage of those front hoofs, the size of three-gallon buckets, high in the air, and tossed his lasso over them. Yanking his paint around he spurred him away, and the big stallion crashed to earth on his side. With the two ropes pulling his neck in two directions and his front feet being pulled a third, the stallion was momentarily helpless.

The three well-trained saddle horses kept the ropes taut as their riders dismounted and rushed to the stallion's head.

"Walt, get the halter," Red shouted as he and Parker dropped on their knees on the stallion's neck!

With his air cut off by the two nooses around his neck, the stallion's struggles became weaker. In seconds, Walt was there with the special halter and in a few more seconds, it was in place on the stricken horses head.

Red fumbled for a remote control to the truck's winch, and the rope to the halter began to tighten.

"He is about out of air," Walt warned and Red and Parker ran to their respective mounts to loosen the lassos. A word to Walt's paint and it obediently move forward to loosen its rope. Walt threw all three nooses off the stallion and stepped away.

The stallion's huge chest heaved as the lungs strained to pull in oxygen. It was several minutes before he was breathing normal. The wranglers were back on their mounts

———

32

with ropes coiled and ready, awaiting the next moves from the big horse.

Slowly the stallion struggled to his feet, where he swayed a bit as his strength returned. At Red's activation with his remote control, the winch slowly tightened the rope leading to the horse halter. The gray attempted to pull back, but the wench inexorably commenced to pull him toward the loading ramp. Step by step, he advanced with the rope so taut, you could play a tune on it. All attempts to rear were thwarted and finally the big gray was tight against the front of the trailer. As a precaution, Walt snapped a short chain on the halter an affixed it to a corner post.

Meanwhile, the frantic mares were crowded against the far side of the corral. Walt rode among them to resume cutting out the good stock and letting them back into the pasture pen.

"Walt, I think I saw a brand on one of those sorrels," Red called out. "If I am right, toss a rope on her, if you get a chance."

Two more mares were cut out before Walt was able to separate the sorrel mare from her mates and confirm that she did indeed, have a brand on her shoulder.

"Boss, she is first class," Walt called out, "and plenty smart. She always makes sure there are two or three horses between her and me. But she's pretty tall so if she sticks her head up, I'll nail her!"

Finally, Red was satisfied that he had all the good quality mares cut out except the branded sorrel. Parker locked the gate panel and mounted his horse. The three wranglers managed to separate her from her mates and Walt roped her.

The sorrel made no attempt to fight, once the noose went around her neck, but docilely followed Walt to the side of the corral where he tied her. Teresa, who had been watching, wide eyed, at the action in the corral, came over to check the sorrel. The mare seemed surprisingly gentle and didn't object to being petted and scratched.

"Let's get the rest of them loaded," cried Red. "Get a count on them."

The presence of the stallion, already loaded into the

stock trailer encouraged the remaining mares, with the three yelling wranglers behind them, to walk up the ramp.

"I counted sixteen, Red," Parker remarked as he closed the gate on the trailer. "Plus seven scrawny yearlings."

Red nodded. He had counted the same.

"You want to ride in with me, Teresa," Red called as he headed for the truck cab.

"Gee, Red. Could I work with this mare? She seems real tame," Teresa responded.

"Red, I think you need to order another mile of fencing," Parker interrupted. "I don't think we have enough to finish the Seeps pen."

Red waved his consent to both of them and drove away, headed for town with his second load of wild horses.

Parker and Walt watched the truck and trailer start up the trail and then at each other.

"Red has a late start," Parker remarked as an excuse for Red's abruptness. "Reckon we have enough material at the Seeps to keep us busy this afternoon."

"Can't dismantle either of the corrals, until we move these mares over to the blue roan," Walt agreed. "There are a couple more herds around here that we could trap. We will take the sorrel with us as she seems to have settled down."

Leading their mounts and Red's black, the two men joined Teresa and the tethered sorrel.

"We are headed for the Seeps to start the corral there," Parker informed her. "You could take Red's horse and go back to camp or ride with us."

"You know, Parker, I would like to go with you guys, but I would like to ride the sorrel," Teresa stated. "I am a very good rider and have ridden bareback a lot." She added at their dubious looks. "We could use Red's bridle and try here in the corral first."

Walt shrugged his shoulders and began to fashion a halter from the end of his lasso to lead the black. Teresa had his okay!

Parker, seeing that he was out numbered, acquiesced. "I ought to ride her first though. She is likely to buck.

"No," Teresa said firmly. "She likes me, I just fed

her an apple. Besides the ground is pretty soft here." She indicated the heavily cut up dirt underfoot. "Won't hurt me, if she does dump me off!"

Walt slid an arm over the black's neck and removed the bridle, replacing it with his improvised halter. The sorrel accepted the bit with little resistance and with some minor adjustments, the sorrel was wearing the bridle.

Without any further comment, Parker cupped his hand for Teresa to step up on and she was astride the sorrel! Teresa urged the mare to a trot and they moved easily around the enclosure. The men unclipped a panel and carried it to one side and Teresa rode out into the open. The sorrel wanted to run, so Teresa loosed the reins and they galloped away to circle and come back to the corral. Teresa tightened the reins a bit on the way back, and the sorrel dropped into a smooth pacing gait.

She was greeted by two wide grins.

"My apology, Teresa," Parker exclaimed. "You don't have to take a back seat to any rider, saddle or bareback. As soon as we get the cooler packed on the black, we will be on our way."

CHAPTER 5

The Lady Is Convinced

Red had phoned his boss, Richard Cooper ahead and Mister Cooper had chosen to meet him at the holding corral.

"You have performed splendidly, Red," he stated, quite unexpectedly. His subordinates were not used to excessive praise for their good work. "I did not expect such rapid progress!"

He shook Red's hand as Red descended from the truck.

"We've had good luck, trapping a herd the first night after completing the corral," Red acknowledged. "Hiring on Wiley was a big bonus. He is exceptional handy with horses. But I don't expect this kind of rapid results in the future!"

Mister Cooper had moved around to look at the trailer load.

"My word! That is a big brute! How did you get a halter on him and get him loaded," he exclaimed.

"It took all three of us to choke him down, throw him and wench him into the trailer," Red replied. "Getting that halter off is going to be a challenge, Boss. Say a prayer for me."

"Why er, yes. Perhaps I will," Mister Cooper replied, unexpectedly, and removed his hat and bowed his head.

"Father, you have blessed this young man with talent and good fortune. Now, please guide his hand as he releases this giant stallion, who was Your creation, and protect both of them from harm. Amen."

Red had climbed upon the truck bed and unfastened the chain that had been a backup for the halter rope. Now only the winch held the big stud to the front of the trailer. He had ceased to pull back on the rope, however.

Several men had stopped to watch, attracted by the size of the stallion. One was carrying a metal hook for lifting hay bales. Red was about to reach inside the trailer to grasp the top of the halter when he spotted the man's hay hook.

"Mister, could I borrow that hook for a minute," he addressed him.

"Sure," the man replied and handed over the hay hook.

Slowly, Red reached into the trailer. The stallion reared back, but Red cautiously eased the hook under the rope behind the horse's ears. When he had it in place, he braced himself and, using the remote, released the winch.

Released, the stallion half fell backward, slamming Red against the trailer fence, but he hung on tightly to the hook, and the halter slid over the horses ears and head, freeing the big horse.

Holding his strained shoulder, Red jumped down from the truck and motioned on of the handlers to open the trailer gate. Within seconds, the trailer was empty.

"Are you okay," Mister Cooper asked anxiously.

"My arm and shoulder took quite a beating," Red replied, "but otherwise, okay." He tossed the hook to its owner. "Thanks a bunch! I would have lost some fingers without it!"

Red and Mister Cooper moved over to a bench, nearby and seated themselves.

"You chose not to leave the Clydesdale on the range," Mister Cooper quizzed Red.

"I didn't think most of your buyers would be looking for draft horses, Boss. Moreover, he is just plain mean and attacked my Quad. There are better stallions out there." Red defended his decision.

Richard Cooper nodded his head without comment.

"That young lady, Miss Castell. How did that work

out?"

"Teresa Castell is still at our camp, Boss. I think she is on our side at this point. She was pretty negative at first, but saw some of her information was erroneous. I think her trip with us has been productive," Red expounded.

Richard Cooper stood up. "Keep up the good work. See you next time."

Red's arm ached as he drove back to camp, and it was late, when he arrived at camp. The others had already eaten their supper.

"I'll heat up your chow, Boss," Walt greeted him.

"We voted to go ahead and eat, Red," Parker apologized. "We were starved!"

"Thanks, Walt. Give me a chance to get the dirt off me. I feel like Mister Sandman!" Red headed for the stream.

As Red was eating, Teresa noticed that he was favoring his right arm.

"You hurt your arm, Red. What happened?"

Red explained his difficulty in removing the halter. "We need to rig a hook and chain to the front of the trailer. I would have lost my fingers, if that guy hadn't come by with that bale hook!"

"Some of the Lord's work," Parker suggested.

"A short chain welded to a bale hook and fastened to the front of the rack ought to do it," Walt suggested. "I can rig up one and you can have it welded next trip."

"Thanks, Walt," Red responded. "We will load up those mares at Willow Creek and tote them over to Raidy's. We'll cut the blue roan's yearlings away from him and turn the rest out. His herd will be a little short, but maybe we can add to it later. I don't want them cleaning off all the grazing at Raidy's Springss."

Teresa had been rummaging around in her Wrangler and returned with a jar of cream.

"This stuff is supposed to do magic things for sore muscles, Red," she proclaimed. "Peel off your shirt and I'll rub some on."

With his supper finished, Red obligingly pulled off his shirt. "How did it go with that sorrel mare? Did you get

———

38

her tamed?"

"Red, she is amazingly gentle," Teresa talked as she massaged Red's sore shoulder. "I rode her around bareback. She has a gait like a rocking chair! I would love to own her."

"Whoa! You rode her and without a saddle!" Red laughed admiringly. "That took some nerve! We'll keep her around and I will ask Mister Cooper. We could haul her in on the next load, or when I go in to pick up that order of fencing."

Teresa finished rubbing on the salve and handed Red his shirt. "Could we take a walk, Red?"

Red nodded and took her hand to head out on the prairie. The sound of the trickling water followed them. Out of earshot and eyesight, Teresa turned to face him.

"Much as I would like to hang around and finish, what we started the other night, I have to go back tomorrow," Teresa began. "It has been a memorable week for me, and I'll not forget you. If you are ever in the vicinity of Laramie, look me up." Teresa passed over her business card. "I have been known to accept invitations to dinner!"

Teresa turned as to go back to camp. Red caught her arm and swung her to him.

"This place will feel like a morgue without you around," he muttered thickly and pressed her to his chest for a long lingering kiss.

Teresa broke away. "Come. We must return to camp!"

Sensing that something was amiss, Parker and Walt merely said good night and retired. Red and Teresa did the same.

Nothing was pressing so the entire camp slept in. The sun was well up, when they sit down to breakfast.

"It's a good thing that I am leaving or I would soon lose my girlish figure," Teresa remarked as she finished off a plate of pancakes, fried eggs and ham.

Parker, who was the cook that morning, started to smile in appreciation, until the first part of her remark sank in.

"You're leaving us," he asked in surprise.

"Yes," Teresa responded reluctantly. "I have already overstayed the time, my boss allowed me. I am hoping that the pictures and information that I have gathered, will appease her!"

"We will sure miss having you around, Teresa," Walt put in. "What are we going to do with that sorrel mare, now?"

"I'm going to check with Mister Cooper, today, to see, what I must do to turn her over to Teresa." Red intervened.

Teresa went into the tent, where she had been sleeping and returned immediately with her bag, which she deposited in her jeep and returned.

She gave each man a hug and a kiss on the cheek.

"You all have treated me like a queen! I will be forever spoiled." She headed for her jeep.

"Wait a minute, Teresa." Parker stepped forward to intercept her. "We need to offer a prayer for your safekeeping."

"Yes, of course," Red agreed.

The four of them knelt for prayer, after which Teresa climbed into her Wrangler and drove away.

CHAPTER 6

The Arrest

The loading and transportation of the mares from the gray stallion to Raidy's Springs was uneventful. The blue roan stallion thanked them for the new harem by racing away at top speed. He would not soon return to that vicinity! The yearlings, which were left behind, neighed their displeasure in vain, but returned to grazing when the others were out of sight.

The Seeps was a good two hour drive from their base camp so the men decided not to attempt any work there that day.

The following day, Parker and Walt took a quad to the Seeps, while Red drove into town, taking the new sorrel mare with him, to pick up additional fencing. A phone call from Mister Cooper had alerted him of its arrival.

As they sat down to supper that evening, Parker brought up a new concern!

"Red, we saw some strange tire tracks today! Someone else is interested in these wild horses," he revealed. "Looked like dune buggy tracks."

"I don't like that," Red responded with a frown. "I'll drive over to the plateau tomorrow. Maybe I can spot them with my scope."

By mid-morning, Red had his telescope in place and was scanning the area. Jana Lake was on the far extreme of his telescope's capability, but he could make out, what appeared to be several RV campers parked in the camping area adjacent the small lake.

Closer at hand, he could see several dust trails. As he watched, one veered off from the others. Red could see it close in on a wild horse herd, causing the herd to stampede. The vehicle quickly overtook the running horses as they entered a dry lakebed, where the ground was smooth and level.

A huge dust cloud arose, obscuring Red's vision as the dune buggy dust trail merged with that of the wild horses. They were closer now and Red saw a single horse emerge from the dust cloud, closely followed by the dune buggy. The driver apparently had singled out one horse, probably the stallion, to pursue!

"That SOB will kill that poor horse, if he doesn't stop," Red muttered furiously. He pounded the ground with his fist in frustration!

He lost sight of the two objects momentarily and, when he regained the picture, the wild horse was down and the dune buggy was speeding away.

So angry, his hands were trembling, Red fumbled for his cell phone. His call produced only an answering machine.

"Boss, this is Red Iverson. I just observed a dune buggy run down a wild horse and possible kill it. I think the buggy came from Jana Lake, where there are several campers parked, and I am going down to talk to them."

Next, Red dialed his co-worker, Parker.

"Parker, I just saw a dune buggy run down a wild horse. He may have killed it. I think it's from Jana Lake and I am on my way over there. Can you and Walt meet me there?"

"Sure, Red. Are you still at the plateau? Let us meet you and drive in together," Parker suggested.

"I don't want to wait, Parker. They might leave. See you over there and check your pistols!" Red hung up to end the discussion.

The smell of barbecue hamburgers was still in the air when Red arrived at the campsites. Three small RVs and a pick-up with a trailer were parked at one site and a larger RV, surrounded by several small tents were at an adjacent site.

Four dune buggies were sitting near the smaller RVs. Red stopped there and, leaving his quad, walked over to the fire. Several couples were standing or sitting nearby, dining on hamburgers and beer.

"You are just in time for a burger, Stranger. Come on over and help yourself," cried the man next to the fire.

"No, thank you, Sir. I am here on business. Red's face was stony, but his voice was courteous. "My name is Iverson. I am a ranger with the Bureau of Land Management. I observed a dune buggy run a horse to death out on the dry lakebed. The buggy came from here. I would like to talk to the driver." Red produced his ranger badge and held it up.

One of the standing men dropped his beer can. The contents slopped over his shoes, but he didn't notice.

"I was only havin a little fun," he quavered. "I didn't mean to hurt him!"

"You run a horse at panic speed, five miles across a sandy desert with ninety degree temperatures, and you didn't think that would hurt him?" Red ground out through clenched teeth!

A woman walked over to the guilty looking one.

"You damned fool, Alec. I told you to let them alone." She berated him. She then turned to Red. "He didn't mean no harm, Mister Ranger. It was just a dumb horse. You guys are killing them off anyhow. What does one more matter?"

A number of people from the larger RV had walked over to hear what was happening. A young woman stepped from among them.

"Is that true? That the government is killing off some of the wild horses," she inquired.

"No, it isn't true, Madam. And would you kindly mind your own business, unless you are a part of this?"

Red's temper went up a notch. He returned his attention to "Alec".

"Let me see your driver's licence," Red directed.

Alec reached into his back pocket, removing his wallet and showed his license to Red.

"Take it out of your wallet, please," Red responded and Alec complied, handing the license to him.

"Alec Willets, you are under arrest! Get anything here that you need. I am taking you into Rawlings. Anything you say may be used against you." Red quoted as an afterthought.

"Wait a minute, Ranger Iverson. Do you have the authority to make arrests," the man, who had initially greeted Red, spoke up.

"Anyone can make a 'Citizen Arrest', Sir," Red answered. "But yes, as a ranger, I am authorized."

Any more conversation was prohibited by the noise of an approaching quad with no mufflers.

Parker pulled up with a flourish and shut off the noisy quad.

"Thought we would give you some warning that we were on our way," Parker grinned as he disembarked.

Red grasped Alec by the arm, above the elbow and turned him toward his quad.

"Let's go," he told him.

Alec took two steps with Red, then shook his arm loose from Red's grasp and gave him a strong push before taking off on a run toward one of the dune buggies. Recovering from the push, Red sprinted after him. He caught him as he was climbing into the driver's seat and yanked him back out.

Alec swung a fist at Red's head, which was avoided, but Red responded with a left hook to Alec's unguarded stomach, which did connect!

"I was hoping you wouldn't do anything stupid," Red said to Alec, who was bent over, gasping for breath. "Now I have to put a rope on you plus charge you with resisting arrest and assaulting an officer."

Anticipating Red's next move, Walt trotted over with a length of rope from his quad and at Red's nod, proceeded to bind Alec's hands behind his back.

The group was silent as the two quads drove away.

CHAPTER 7

Man Down

"I turned him over to the Sheriff's Department," Red finished relating the episode to Mister Cooper. "And charged him with reckless driving, destroying public property, and cruelty to animals, resisting arrest and assault. I didn't know all the legal language, so left it with them to sort it out."

"You know, Red, that you can't prove, who was driving that dune buggy, don't you," Richard Cooper asked.

"I know, Boss, but I just couldn't let it go without doing something. Maybe the judge will convict him of assaulting me." Red looked very discouraged. "And maybe the public will be on our side for a change."

"Anything more you want to add to the tape, Red?"

"No, Sir. I think that covers it," Red replied.

"Fine. I will turn this over to our legal department. Off record, Red, I don't see that you had any other option, but don't expect much." Richard Cooper stood up. "You will probably be required to speak with our attorney and testify. I will call you when I know something."

The three wranglers were quiet that night over supper. Parker finally broke the silence.

"Well, the Seeps is fenced, Red, and I had an idea. Why don't we bring those roan yearlings over to our corral, we have plenty of hay. We could even tame them down a

---

bit; maybe break them to the halter. What do you think? It would free up all three traps!"

"Once we get them in the trailer, I could put halters on them," Walt added. "I could work with them during the day, as there won't be much to do except staying up nights, until we catch another herd."

"We could just pull up the loading corral at the Raidy's Springs and stack the panels nearby," Parker argued. "There have been herds wanting to get in there for water."

"Well, if Walt got them halter broke, we could just lead them to their new herd," Red mused. "Wouldn't really need to load them up here. Good idea, Parker. We'll do it. Tomorrow morning we load up the yearlings and dismantle the loading corral."

"Boss, if we shorten the gate panels to ten feet, one man could handle them easily," Walt added. "We could watch all three corrals at the same time."

"Are you guys good with staying up all night and sleeping days," Red inquired.

"Gee, I don't know, Red," Parker said doubtfully. "You can't smoke, can't read or listen to the radio! Can't even move around to stay awake or talk to anyone on the phone. I never been good at that!"

"So! The worst scenario; a herd of wild horses come in and get a drink without being caught!" Walt was eager to try it.

"We'll try it," Red decided. "I like the idea of having three chances to trap a herd. Let's get some shut-eye."

The morning and early afternoon were spent dismantling the loading pen at Raidy's Springs and constructing smaller panels to use as gates. It was decided to each pick a herd near-by and gently push them toward their respective traps before retiring to the base camp and attempting to get some sleep. They set their alarms to awaken at midnight, hoping to catch the wild horses as they watered after dawn.

Fortified with thermos bottles of black coffee and some snacks, three groggy wranglers set out to their assigned watering hole during the early morning hours. They were to return to camp at eight o'clock.

Red, being the closest to camp at Raidy's Springs, was the first to arrive back at camp and had coffee and a ham and egg omelet ready to toss in the skillet when the others straggled in.

"No horses came around Raidy's Springs yesterday," he remarked, as the others arrived.

"Tracks showed the wild ones were in for water at Willow Creek during the evening," Walt reported.

"I told you," Parker admitted, remorsefully. "I woke up as they were leaving. Nice bunch of mares. The stallion had already got by me. Didn't look like the bunch I eased over there, though."

"Never mind, Parker. We'll both sit out there tonight. Would have been nice to catch another bunch, though," Red said regretfully.

"Boss, I saw the sun reflect on a glass up on Lonesome Mesa, when I was coming back. Someone is watching us," Walt warned. "Don't suppose someone is interested in our catching some wild horses?"

Halting in the middle of dumping the omelet in the hot skillet, Red looked up in surprise.

"Why would anyone be keeping track of us?"

"There are a lot of people with strong feelings about these wild horses, Boss," Walt offered. "From those who want to just kill off the herds to those that want them untouched and unsupervised. None of them seem to trust the Bureau or the statistics that we put out."

"I suppose so," Red replied as he flipped the omelet. "We might have to put one of us up on the Mesa to keep track of, what is going on."

"Breakfast's ready," Red added. "We will try to get five or six hours sleep then push some herds toward the corrals again and be hid out before dark this time."

Walt had a bunch of ham and cheese sandwiches made plus a large pot of coffee ready when Red and Parker awoke about one o'clock. Red and Parker took one quad and headed toward the Seeps while Walt went back to Willow Creek. Raidy's Springs was left unattended.

———

Red and Parker herded two bunches of wild horses toward the Seeps before hiding the quad and stationing themselves near the opening to await a herd coming to water.

As they were approaching the blind, Red's cell phone rang. It was Richard Cooper.

"Red, you need to be present at a hearing on Friday at ten o'clock. Can you be there?"

"Yes, Sir. I'll be there," Red replied.

"See you then," Mister Cooper hung up without further comment.

"Got to be at a hearing on Friday," Red mentioned to Parker.

"Maybe we will have a load of horses by then," Parker said with a grin.

By sundown, the two wranglers were in hiding in a blind near the entrance to the corral. Both herds of wild horses were working their way toward the Seeps. Parker was already dozing, with his hat over his eyes. Red cast a short prayer heavenward for a successful evening as the light failed. As his eyes became accustomed to the starlight, he could easily make out the coral entrance, but his view of the wild horses faded into darkness.

The desert gets chilly at night and Red wrapped an Indian blanket around his shoulders and laid one over the sleeping Parker. He then opened his thermos of coffee and poured a cupful.

"I wonder how the hearing will develop," he mused. "Somehow, I feel that I will end up as the bad guy."

Red strove to pull his mind away from that subject and focused on the job at hand. He gazed jealously at his sleeping partner.

"All Parker has to do is quit moving his feet, and he falls asleep," he grinned to himself. "I'll wake him about midnight."

Red was on his fourth cup of coffee, when he became aware of horses moving nearby. He could just make out a dark blob moving steadily toward the corral. Soft snorts sounded as the horses cleared the dust from their nostrils.

Carefully, he set down his coffee cup and reached over to rouse Parker. He held one hand close to Parker's mouth to stifle any noise that he might make as he awakened. It wasn't needed, as Parker woke silently. Together, they waited as the blob drew closer and individual animals could be discerned.

One animal, probably the stallion, stopped briefly at the entrance to the trap with a loud snort and then breaking into a trot, he led his harem into the corral and headed for the water.

Aware that the slightest sound could bring the herd racing back to the opening, the two men carefully began to carry the gates into place. This was done without mishap and they retired to their hiding place to await the horse's reaction when they discovered the blocked entrance.

They waited about a half hour before the horse herd was heard returning. With their bellies full of water, the herd was taking their time, nipping an occasional tuft of grass. When reaching the fence, there was considerable milling around and snorting, but they finally dispersed and commenced to lay down to sleep.

Quietly, Red and Parker eased from their hideout and walked to the quad. With headlights dimmed and at the engine barely turning over, they drove from the site and on toward their camp.

After congratulating each other and a saying a short prayer of thanks to their Creator, they discussed joining Walt at Willow Creek.

"We can't call him, he might have his phone on loud," Red remarked. "If we drive over there and scare off a herd, he'll kill us!"

"He was hot to go it alone," Parker agreed. "Best leave well enough alone."

They arrived at base camp around midnight, satisfied with their day's results.

Red was the first to waken and had hot cakes and ham frying when Parker stirred. The sun was just peeking over the horizon.

"What's the hurry?" muttered a sleepy wrangler. "We got nothing special to do except build the loading corral at the Seeps.

"I'm concerned about Walt. He hasn't come in yet," Red replied.

"Aw! He probably just fell asleep," Parker averred.

"Well, come over and stuff yourself. We are driving over there ASAP," Red replied, pouring a cup of coffee for his friend.

Finishing their breakfast, the two filled a thermos of fresh coffee for Walt and headed out for Willow Creek.

Red was driving fairly fast and a particular large pothole caused Parker to crack his knee on the dashboard!

"Ouch!" he bawled out. "Take it easy, Red. Walt's fine."

Red slowed down slightly, but continued at a fast pace until Willow Creek was in sight.

Arriving at the corral at chaotic scene spread out before them! Several of the small panels that they were using as a gate were strewn around the entrance! The closest one to the solid fence lay on top of a fallen figure!

Red braked the Quad to a stop and Parker was out of the vehicle, before it stopped moving. He had the panel off the inert figure, when Red dropped to his knees beside his friend. Walt lay crumpled up on his back. A trickle of dried blood ran from his mouth, his face was ashen! A large purple lump was above his left eye!

"He is still breathing," Red cried. "Call nine-one-one. Ask them to send a chopper out. I think Walt is bad hurt!"

As Parker was conversing with the emergency operator, Red trotted to the Quad and retrieved a blanket. He laid it over his unconscious friend.

"Please, Lord, let Walt be all right," Red pleaded, his throat thick.

Meanwhile, Parker was repeating back to the operator, "Right, don't move him, especially his head. Keep him warm and a damp cloth on his brow. Helicopter is on its way. Thank you."

Parker hung up his phone and wiped his damp face. Red already had a canteen out and was soaking a handkerchief to lay on Walt's forehead. With his hand still on Walt's forehead, Red offered up a prayer for his recovery.

51

"Lord, I don't know, what all is injured or broken on Walt, but You do. He is Your child, Lord and I know You don't want him to suffer either, so I just pray You will heal his hurts quickly. Amen!"

There didn't seem to be anything that they could do, while awaiting the arrival of the chopper.

"Let's use a panel and a blanket to shade him from the sun," Parker suggested.

"Good idea," Red replied.

The two of them made short work of pounding two posts into the ground and attaching a panel. A blanket was thrown over the panel to shade the injured man. Red pulled out his cell phone and placed a call to Mister Cooper, leaving a message on the recorder.

To the waiting men, it seemed like ages, but in a very short time, the sound of an approaching helicopter reached them. It was a windless morning and the plane came straight in to hover near where the Quad was parked. A dense cloud of dust rose from around the swirling blades, as the vehicle settled to the desert floor, and the engine was shut down. Two men jumped from the helicopter and rushed to the injured man's side. A third man followed with a stretcher.

"His heart is beating strong," one of the paramedics muttered.

"Neck isn't broken, but some ribs are and possibly the collar bone," the other added. "That lump on his head looks bad! We'll put a splint on that broken arm and get him on the stretcher."

"Let me stabilize his neck, just in case," the first one interjected.

The three paramedics carefully lifted Walt's inert body, laid him on the stretcher, and carried him to the plane.

"I'm sorry that we don't have room for either of you," one man, apparently the pilot, said to Red. "We will fly him straight to Rawlings Central Hospital."

The two wranglers watched the helicopter disappear, than Red turned to his partner.

"Let's see if we can decipher what happened."

"The connectors are twisted and broken on these two panels," Parker reported.

"Same with this one. Looks like, he had all the panels up, except the one he was carrying, when the herd hit him. Those horses were running flat out! He is lucky to be alive!" Red shook his head.

They put away the four small panels and drove back to their camp.

"I know you would like to go with me, Parker," Red explained, "but I need you to take care of our horses here, and we need that loading pen built at the Seeps. We have to load that herd up, or turn them loose again. There isn't enough graze to feed that herd too long."

Sure, Red, I'll take care of things," Parker assured him. "You look after Walt."

CHAPTER 8

Walt's Story

Richard Cooper was in the waiting room and greeted Red, when he arrived at the hospital.

"Walt is pretty badly beaten up, Red, with two broken ribs, his left arm and collar bone. The worst is that lump on his head. The doctors think there might be brain damage and aren't encouraging him to awaken." Mister Cooper took a couple paces up and back. "His sister is with him now and his younger brother is on his way here. Both parents are dead."

Red shook his head sadly. "It's my fault. He shouldn't have been out there by himself. It takes too long for one person to get the gate in place, and the horses must have heard--!"

"It wasn't anybody's fault," his employer interrupted. "Accidents happen, when you work with wild animals! You just put that thought out of your mind. You go in and talk to his sister. Tell her not to worry about expenses. It will all be taken care of, and he will get the best specialist available. I need to get back to my office and write an accident report. Come up, when you can and fill me in on the details."

With a pat on Red's shoulder, Richard Cooper turned to leave.

"Thanks, Boss, I'll be up shortly," Red smiled weakly

and followed him to the door.

A young man was entered and started down the hall behind Red. Red glanced at him and then stopped.

"You look a lot like Walt. You wouldn't be his brother, would you," Red asked. "I'm Red Iverson."

The young man stopped beside him. "Yes, I'm Ben Wiley, Walt's brother," he said with a half-smile.

"I'm on my way to see Walt," Red stated. "Mind if I walk with you?"

Ben nodded and the two men proceeded down the hall, stopping at the ICU ward. The nurse on duty looked up as the approached her desk.

"You are here to see Walt Wiley," she inquired.

"Yes, Ma'am. I'm his brother. Is he awake?" Ben's tone was almost pleading.

"I'm sorry. The doctor doesn't want him to wake up as yet. It helps the brain to heal." The nurse was very sympathetic. "Your sister is with him, he is in the first cubical. Go on in. We ask that there be no more than three visitors at a time, but as long you stay relatively quiet, I can waive that. He is our only patient, for now."

Beth Wiley was barely out of her teens. Slim, with a dusky complexion set off by a red blouse and fawn colored skirt, she was very easy to look at. She stood up at their entrance and hugged her brother.

"This is Red Iverson, Walt's boss," Ben introduced when Beth stepped back. "My sister, Beth."

Red transferred his hat to his left hand from his right hand and held it out to Beth, who took it shyly.

"I was more like a co-worker than a boss," Red declared without releasing her hand. "Our real boss, Richard Cooper, asked me to relate to you that all Walt's expenses will be taken care of and that no cost will be spared to get your brother the best of doctors and care!"

"Thank you," Beth replied brokenly. "It is so hard to see him lying there, all helpless. He was always so virile and strong. Like he could do anything. He is the only parent Ben and I have had, the last eight years."

"Don't give up hope, Beth. Just keep praying that God will heal him," Red responded. "Walt is tough and

---

55

strong. He will come through this."

Red released Beth's hand and stepped over to Walt' bed. He laid his hand gently on Walt's unbandaged arm.

"Come on, pard! It isn't time for you to go! You get yourself up and come back to work. We need you," he whispered quietly to the comatose figure and then, with a nod, good-by, to the siblings, Red strode from the ward.

After telling Richard Cooper as many details as he knew, Red left his office and drove to the Wrangler Inn, a small motel ran by an elderly couple. As he approached the desk, his cell phone rang.

"Red, is that you," a feminine voice inquired.

"Hi, Teresa. Yes, it's me." Red recognized her voice. "How are you?"

"Oh, Red, I've been so worried! I heard one of you was trampled by wild horses. Who was it and is he going to be okay," Teresa inquired.

"It was Walt, Teresa. He was trying to close the opening and got caught like I almost did. He was by himself and we found him the next morning. He received a hard knock on the head and is still unconscious. Also has broken ribs and collarbone. The doc is afraid of brain damage, but it is too soon to tell," Red replied.

"Red, my boss wants me to drive up and get a story to follow up on my last one. Could you get me a room near or where you're staying? I will be late getting in," she asked.

"I'm at the Wrangler Inn, next to the highway," Red answered. "Hang on a minute. I'll get you a room number." To the elderly lady behind the desk. "Do you have a single for my friend? She will be late getting in."

The lady held up a key. "Number four. If she comes in after ten PM, the key will be in the door. She can check in the morning." The lady spoke quite loud.

"Did you hear that, Teresa? Yes, key in the door of number four, if you get in after ten." Red relayed and hung up his phone.

"Her name is Teresa Castell. She works for a magazine in Laramie. I'll need a room, too. Not sure how long. My partner got trampled by wild horses and is still out of it." Red laid his credit card on the counter.

———

With his suitcase carried to his room, Red called the hospital. He was transferred to the ICU. The nurse gave him over to Ben.

"Hi, Ben. This is Red. Any change in Walt?"

"No. No change. The doctor was in, though, and thought he could detect a slight reduction in the swelling of his head," Ben replied.

"I don't reckon you two have had anything to eat. Could you meet me at Ginger's Deli for supper or I could pick up some sandwiches and bring them up. I haven't eaten since breakfast," Red declared.

There was a silence as the two siblings conferred.

"Beth doesn't want to leave here," Ben came back on the line. "Some ham and cheese on rye would be great!"

"Done. I'll be there shortly," Red replied. "Pepsi okay for drinks?"

At Ben's okay, Red left the room for his truck.

All of the diners were hungry so there was little conversation, as they consumed the half dozen sandwiches, Red had brought. Afterward, Red related, how they had been operating and their purpose in doing it. He stressed Walt's part and told of his admiration of Walt's ability to handle horses.

Ben's face glowed as he listened.

"You should watch him work at taming the wild ones. He seems to be able to communicate with them in an extraordinary way," Ben extolled. "Some of his friends kiddingly call him 'The Horse Whisperer'!"

Red soon found himself fighting to stay awake.

"I only got a few hours of sleep last night and it's been a long day," Red stated. "Do you have a place to sleep here?"

"They will let Beth sleep in the adjoining bed, and I'll roll up in some blankets on the floor," Ben replied.

Red nodded his agreement.

"There will be a lady here tomorrow to do a story on Walt; what he did before working with me, etc. She spent a week with us and is very sympathetic with the wild horse situation." Red stood up to leave. "Her name is Teresa

Castell. I think you will like her."

Red woke late with someone pounding on his door.

"Red, are you dead? Wake up!" Red recognized the voice of Teresa Castell.

"All right! All right, I'm awake. What's the big rush," Red growled groggily.

"Cuz I'm starved! I didn't get any dinner last night. I'll take you to breakfast if you will be ready in fifteen minutes," Teresa replied.

"Okay, but I may have to only shave half of my face," Red answered.

"Forget the shave, just toss on some fufu juice to kill the odor and let's go." Teresa was walking away as she spoke.

Over coffee, while they awaited their meal, Red related the details leading up to Walt's accident.

"Walt was hot to man all three traps, but I should have vetoed it. There should always be another guy around, when you're working with wild horses. Walt was always so self-sufficient, it was hard to hold him back," Red explained remorsefully.

"Don't take it personal, Red. You don't know the whole story, yet," Teresa rebutted. "Wait until Walt wakes up and tells us the rest of the story!"

Their breakfast arrived at that point and conversation lagged. Red pushed his empty plate back and dialed the hospital between sips of coffee.

"Good morning, Ben. Have you had breakfast?"

"Good morning, Red. Yeah, they sent up food for us. Pretty darn good, too," Ben answered. "Doctor says that Walt is just sleeping now and should wake up in a few hours. He seemed more optimistic today than yesterday."

"If you feel like talking, I have Teresa with me and she would like to meet you all and see Walt," Red suggested.

"Sure. Bring her up. I can talk about Walt for hours." Ben laughed.

After introductions, Teresa settled back in a chair with her IPad on her lap.

58

"Just tell me what you want me to know and I will sort it out later," she told Ben. "And, Beth, throw in your two-bits anytime, also."

"Walt wasn't the typical Indian buck that was happy to hang around the reservation living off the government," Ben began. "He was in line for the tribal council, but disagreed with the old ones, who espoused keeping the tribe together. Walt felt like we should go out and learn a trade, how to fend for ourselves and become like any other American citizen. He is fiercely independent and resents getting money that he did not earn!"

"Walt enlisted the Marine Corps, when he turned eighteen and joined an infantry battalion at Camp Pendleton. His ease of slipping around the "enemy" troops, especially at night earned him the nickname of "Injun Joe". In a mock war between two battalions, he went on a solo reconnaissance mission. He slipped into the enemy's headquarters section and tagged, "killed", the entire group, including the battalion commander. He also captured the radio operator with his radio intact and brought him back to his company commander."

"He extracted the enemy code and call signs from the radio operator and, with the commander's help, succeeded in sitting up an ambush for an enemy company and destroying it. This became a pivotal point in which his battalion won the "war". "Walt was promoted to Corporal for his actions!"

"Later in Iraq, then Sergeant Wiley, he did a repeat performance under actual combat conditions. Leading a platoon under a Second Lieutenant on a patrol sweep of a town, they were ambushed by a superior enemy force, hidden in houses. Their platoon was completely surrounded and taking heavy rifle, machine gun and mortar fire, when Walt made his way into the enemy's lines. He deposed the first machine gun nest and, then, discarding his own rifle, he used the enemy rifle and ammunition to clear a path for his men to escape."

Teresa, who had been typing furiously, raised her hand as Ben stopped for breath.

"I don't understand. Why discard his own rifle and use the enemy's?"

"The American rifle makes a distinct sound, easily discernible from the ones the Iraqis use. They would have known immediately that an American was in their midst, if he had used his own weapon," Ben replied.

Teresa nodded her head in understanding and resumed typing.

"Walt rejoined his comrades and carried a badly wounded one to safety in spite of having two minor bullet wounds, himself." Ben resumed. "He was awarded a Silver Star for his action! It read 'for extraordinary skill and valor in extracting his men from a dangerous situation'. He also was promoted to staff sergeant. This was on Walt's second tour in Iraq, and he was released from active duty soon after that, in spite of the Corps effort to keep him. He was offered a Warrant Officer's commission, if he would stay!"

"Our parents were killed in an auto accident, while he was overseas," Beth interrupted. "He came back to take care of us. I don't see how we could have made it without him!" Her voice shook.

Teresa paused in her typing and gazed in awe at the comatose figure. Her mind flashed back to the figure on horseback, deftly dropping a rope over the rearing stallion's legs, then rushing in fearlessly to place the halter over that huge head with its gaping jaws. Yes, that could be the same man!

At this point, Red's cell phone jingled. Red was in a slight shock; he had known none of this. He answered the phone.

"Red, I know this is a bad time, but you are due at the hearing in forty five minutes." It was Richard Cooper.

"Thanks for the head's up, Boss. I had forgotten all about that," Red replied. "I'll head over there shortly."

The phone rang again, as Red slipped it back into his pocket. It was Parker.

"Hi Red. How is Walt doing?"

"About the same, Parker. Doc says he is just sleeping now and is showing some improvement."

"Well, you don't have to worry about the new herd," Parker growled. "Some horse lovers opened the entrance and let them out, last night!"

"Whaat!" Red almost yelled, but held it just in time!

"Yes. They left some tracks, which I have preserved. I am driving in for a couple hours this afternoon. Tell you more when I see you." Parker rang off.

Red sighed as he put his phone away. "I'll be back after the hearing. Probably won't be too long."

He took another look at Walt and walked out.

Red had barely got to his seat, before the presiding judge entered.

"My name is Judge Morgan. This is an informal hearing to ascertain, whether there is enough evidence available for a formal trial. Witnesses will be sworn in; however, certain formalities will be waived."

The judge consulted a paper in front of him. "I call Ranger Curtis Iverson."

Red told his story calmly and coldly until he started describing the stallion's running from the dune buggy. His love for horses became apparent as his voice thickened, when the horse finally fell.

"I followed the vehicle with my telescope back to Jana Lake," Red continued. "We confirmed later, that the stallion was dead."

Red went on relating his confrontation with Alec and his subsequent arrest! The judge asked for clarification on a couple points and told him to step down.

"Alec Willets, take the stand," the judge said next."

"Although this is an informal hearing, Mister Willets, anything you say can be used against you, should a trail be held," the judge informed him after he had been sworn in.

"Do you wish to testify?"

"Yes, Your Honor, I do. It happened, just like the Ranger said," Alec confessed. "It was a stupid thing to do, but I never considered that I was hurting the horse, or that I might kill him. I'm really sorry!"

The judge stared in surprise at the defendant, and then turned to the man's attorney. "Were you aware of, what your client was going to say?"

"Yes, Your Honor, I was. I attempted to dissuade him, but he insisted," the attorney stood up and replied.

"Alec Willets, I have no choice, but to remand you over for trail," the judge ruled. "However it turns out, I commend your honesty. Court dismissed."

Red walked out of the courtroom in shock!

CHAPTER 9

Ben Gets a Job

Teresa was reading aloud from her iPad when Red entered the hospital room. He quietly sought a chair without greetings.

"-unable to back away from danger, Walt faced the horses herd, that was thundering down on him as he had faced danger in past; head on and determined to stop the escaping animals. The wild horses, undeterred by Walt's yells, and the fence panel that he carried, swept over him like a flash flood of rain water down a narrow gulley!"

"The dust, which was stirred up from the racing hooves, slowly settled and the star-lit sky looked down on the crumpled figure. His body, crushed and beaten by the pounding hooves, lay in the dust, awaiting succor from his buddies!"

"Now Walt waits his Heavenly Father's will. Will he be called to his home in heaven or rise up from his hospital bed and again ride in the desert, which he loved? Will God listen to the many prayers of his siblings and friends, or does He have His own plan?"

"We wait!"

Teresa looked up from her iPad. Beth was sobbing quietly.

"That was beautiful, Miss Castell! Thank you!" Beth crossed the room to give Teresa a small hug.

"You're going to put that in a newspaper, Miss Castell?" This from Ben.

"It should go in the Laramie Examiner tomorrow," Teresa smiled. "If I am real lucky, it will be picked up by United Press for a larger distribution."

Suddenly an almost inaudible sound came from the bed.

"Oh!" Beth rushed back to Walt's bedside. "Is he waking up?"

Silence fell a crossed the room and all eyes focused on Walt. His eyes fluttered briefly before springing open. They gazed vacantly around. His lips worked, but they made no sound.

Beth placed a glass of water and a straw to his lips. Walt sucked greedily for a few seconds before his eyes closed again. He seemed to fall back asleep.

Ben ran over to the nurse's station. "Nurse, Nurse! My brother woke up."

With her stethoscope, the nurse listened to his heart and breathing. "His heartbeat is strong; I think that he is just sleeping. I'll let the doctor know." She returned to her station.

Slowly the watchers relaxed, as there were no more signs of Walt waking up, but the atmosphere in the room grew noticeably more hopeful.

After a few minutes, Ben turned to Red. "What was the hearing about and was the outcome to your liking?"

"Yes, Red," Teresa chipped in. "Tell us about it!"

"Well, it started when I was up on Lonesome Mesa, looking for herd locations," Red began. "You remember that look-out point, Teresa." At Teresa's nod, he continued, "I saw this dune buggy chasing a wild horse herd."

Red went to relate the circumstances around the slain stallion and Alec's arrest, the trip to jail and the events at the hearing.

"You could have knocked me over with a feather," Red finished. "That was the last thing I expected from that big ape!"

"So what happens now," Ben asked. He had been listening intently.

—

"I guess there will be a trail," Red replied. "I can probably locate some of the other campers at the lake, that day to corroborate my accusation of his resisting arrest, but without Alec's confession, there is no way that I could prove who was driving that dune buggy!"

"But they can use his confession, can't they?" Ben was persistent.

"I guess so, Ben. I'm not too knowledgeable about court procedures," Red confessed. "And I'm not quite as hot to see him punished, as I was before he spoke up!"

"Ah, Mister Iverson," Ben began.

"Just call me, Red," Red interrupted.

"Red," Ben started over, "it is going to be some time before Walt can work again."

"That's true," Red agreed. "Even if he doesn't have any repercussions from that knock on his skull, that collar bone will take a while to heal."

"So, you're going to need another rider, while Walt is getting well again," Ben reasoned.

"Hey, Ben! Are you hitting me up for a job," Red grinned.

"Yes, I am, Red! I'm not as good with horses as my brother, but I'm better than most. Besides, if you hire somebody else, you'll feel bad when Walt gets well and you have to let that other fellow go," Ben persisted. "This way, my brother gets well and I quit. No hard feelings!"

"Can you cook, Ben?" Red was chuckling now.

"Cook? Of course, I can cook!" Ben was a little nettled as he was beginning to think, Red wasn't taking him seriously.

"Tell you what, Ben," Red was still grinning and he slapped Ben on the shoulder. "If you can bake biscuits as good as your brother, you're hired!"

"You won't be disappointed in either of Ben's riding or his cooking," Beth spoke up. "Walt taught him both!"

Parker chose that moment to quietly enter the room.

"How's Walt doing," he whispered to Red.

"They think that he is out of his coma and just sleeping now," Red answered him in a normal voice. "Do you know Ben and Beth, Walt's brother and sister?"

"Saw Ben riding in the rodeo last summer," Parker replied as he shook hands with Ben. "You did pretty good, if I remember right!"

"He came in third for the 'All Around Champion Cowboy'." Beth answered for him proudly.

"Aw, that's like being third best man at a wedding!" Ben was plainly disgruntled about the subject.

"Say, Walt told me that he had a sister, but I had no idea she was this lovely!" Parker stepped over to take Beth's hand.

"I say, Parker. When you are finished shining up to Miss Wiley, don't forget me!" Teresa entered the conversation.

"Come on, Teresa. You know that I love only you!" Parker crossed the room to give Teresa a bear hug.

Everyone was chuckling by this time at Parker's antics.

"So do we know anything about Walt, yet?" Parker was instantly serious.

Red waved his hand at the sleeping figure. "He woke up briefly and sipped some water. The nurse seems to think he is doing well."

The nurse was looking a bit unhappy with so many visitors, so Red left the ICU and followed Parker into the waiting room. Parker sat down in a chair, next to Red. He slipped out his smart phone.

"Look at these pictures, Red!

The pictures were of small boot tracks in the soft sand.

"These were next to the entrance, where the gate panels were dragged," Parker stated.

"Either a young boy or a girl's boot," Red remarked.

"Not a boy, but a tall girl. Look at the length of her stride." Parker showed a second image.

"I assumed, it would be one of Alec's buddies getting even for his arrest," Red remarked. "But, a girl turning out the wild horses, puts a different slant on things."

"You mentioned a girl at the Lake, half accusing you of killing off the wild horses," Parker reminded him. "Could this be her?"

"I'm a little vague," Red replied. "I was concentrating on Alec and his crowd. But, yes, my impression was, that she was tall for a girl."

Red stood up. "I need to talk to my boss about this." They returned to the ICU.

"Ben, we will hang around town until Walt wakes up." Red continued, "I have a good feeling, now. Just keep praying. You have my cell phone number, call me with any change! Teresa, email me your story, please. I only heard the last part! Come on, Parker."

CHAPTER 10

Guilty Lady

The rising sun spread long shadows across the landscape as the two men used field glasses to sweep over the area. The object of their search was wild horse herds. One of them discarded his field glasses in favor of a large telescope.

Red crouched behind the telescope, which he directed at Jana Lake, far to the west.

"Several motor homes in the camp site," he directed at his partner.

"Well, Red, there are horses hanging out near all three of our pens," Parker replied. "Take your pick."

"We'll ease a couple of bunches toward the Seeps." Red started to pack up the telescope. "But first, let's drive out to the lake and see if we can find the owner of the boots that made those tracks out there."

The smell of breakfast cooking filled the air, as the two wranglers parked the quad and climbed out. Three motor homes were parked in a cluster, and several people were in line, dishing out food to the others.

"Plenty of food here, strangers! You're welcome to join us for breakfast," an older man called out as the wranglers approached.

"Thank you, Sir. We would appreciate a cup of coffee," Red spoke up before Parker could accept.

The older man waved them over to a large coffee urn and proceeded to pour them each a cup.

"I'm Reverend Fallon. This is our second year group. We are here for ten days of Bible Study and to refresh our souls." The man's arm encircled the group.

A young lady stepped forward to join them.

"This is my daughter, Irene," the Reverend introduced her.

"I've met this man before, Dad." Irene stated somewhat nervously. "This is Ranger Iverson. I met him when I was here last week, checking out the area for you."

Red recognized her immediately as the young lady who had quizzed him about killing wild horses. He grinned!

"Ah, yes. You are the lady that thinks all rangers are wild horse killers!"

Irene flushed. "I didn't say that!"

"Tut, tut! What brings you here this morning, Ranger Iverson," Reverend Fallon intervened.

Red set is coffee carefully down on the edge of the table and drew his cell phone from his pocket. He brought up a close-up picture of a set of boot tracks.

"I'm looking for the owner of a special pair of boots," Red responded. "Notice how the owner leans slightly to the left as she walks. The left heel is worn down on the outside, while the right heel is not!" Red changed the picture. "Notice the length of her stride. She is a relatively tall lady."

The Reverend looked puzzled. "Why would you be looking here for those boots, Ranger Iverson?"

Irene Fallon looked down at her tell-tail tracks. Guilt spread across her face! She started to speak.

"Please, Miss Fallon. Would you call this number and talk to this lady?" Red interrupted, handing her a scrap of paper. "Her name is Teresa Castell, and, until a couple weeks ago, she felt the same as you do. She works for a magazine in Laramie and loves horses!"

Irene, grateful not to be questioned about the boot tracks, started to speak, but then, slipped her phone from its case on her belt and walked away from the group, while dialing Teresa's number.

Red picked up his coffee and turned back to Reverend

Fallon. "What church are you from, Reverend?"

Reverend Fallon, who was about to pursue the subject of the boot track, wisely dropped the subject and replied to Red's question.

"Actually, it is the Crossroads Bible College in Laramie. We try to get away for ten days each year during the summer," the reverend explained. "It is very helpful in breaking the ice and in helping the students get better acquainted. There is something about studying God's Word, out and away from houses and people, that makes everything more real!"

"So they are all studying to be preachers," Parker spoke for the first time.

"No, not necessarily," Reverend Fallon replied. "Most just want a college education without the secular distractions of the regular college. What do you young men do?"

"Our job is to see to the well-being of the wild horse herds in this area," Parker answered with a grin.

At the Reverend's bewildered expression, Red added. "There is not enough grazing to support the huge number of horses in this area and we are trapping some and hauling them to better pastures. They are offered practically free to the American public. If we don't get them thinned enough, likely we will have to haul hay to them this winter."

Reverend Fallon nodded. "Very commendable work! We have owned a horse or two most of my life. My daughter, Irene, has developed an almost unreasonable love for them. I hope that boot track business had nothing to do with her."

"Just our little joke, Reverend. Thank you so much for the coffee. I hope you all have a pleasant stay." Red replaced the coffee cup and headed for the quad with Parker at his heels.

Irene intercepted them and placed her hand on Red's arm. "I feel so ashamed with what I did. Miss Castell explained about your work and the dilemma the Bureau faces regarding the wild horse herds. Please forgive me and thank you for not telling Dad that I released those horses!"

"You are forgiven, Miss Fallon," Red assured her. "It took a lot of guts to do what you did and you thought you were doing something good!"

"Well, I owe you a dinner for not telling Dad!" Irene handed Red a scrap of paper. "Call me up when you get to Laramie!"

CHAPTER 11

Ben Proves Himself

With Parker behind the wheel, the quad headed for the Seeps.

"Hey! Did Miss Fallon just leave you her phone number and an invitation to take her to dinner," Parker exclaimed.

"That she did, and I intend to take her up on it; first chance I get," Red replied. "That is some exciting lady!"

"I thought you and Teresa Castell had something going, until I saw her with Walt. She has him in the corral and tied down, waiting on the branding iron." Parker chuckled at his own wit.

"Well, I think that writing that story about him woke her up to what a real man Walt is. Walt doesn't seem to mind either," Red agreed with a smile. "I can't believe, how fast he came out of that coma and without any of his brains scattered, after that kick in the head."

"It is a good thing Walt has those broken bones," Parker averred. "He would be out on his horse by now. Ben told me that the doctor still wants to do a brain scan on a weekly basis for a while. He said sometimes the injury shows up later."

"Well, Ben should be in tomorrow," Red replied. "Let's see if we can move this horse herd closer to the Seeps, so they will water there tonight."

The two wranglers spent the night hid out by the Seeps, but there was no attempt by the wild horses to enter the corral. At dawn, they returned to the camp in disgust! They curled up in their bedrolls to get a few hours of solid sleep before staying out another night.

Red woke with the sun at its zenith and shining full on his face. The smell of frying sausage permeated the noon air. He open his eyes to behold Ben, busily engaged in the camp kitchen.

Ben saw Red sit up in his blankets. "Good morning, boss, or good afternoon. Breakfast will be ready in about fifteen minutes. Just have to make the gravy."

Red gave a kick to Parker's still form as he passed him on the way to the stream to wash and soon they sat down to a meal of omelet and biscuits and sausage gravy.

"Just as good as Walt's," proclaimed Parker as he reached over and speared his fourth biscuit.

Ben grinned his appreciation and began to clean up. "What's on the agenda for the rest of the day, Boss?"

"I was thinking about taking both quads, and driving over to Raidy's Springs and moving several herds toward there. Walt was working with those three colts here, trying to tame them, Ben, would you like to spend some time with them, while we are gone," Red asked. "I'll swing back and pick you up before dark and we will baby-sit that corral tonight."

When Red and Parker returned, Ben had three blankets and thermoses of coffee waiting for them.

"Fixed some sandwiches for us while we are waiting," Ben answered their inquiring looks. "Gonna be chilly tonight, too!"

"Thanks, Ben. That was thoughtful." Red touched Ben's shoulder.

"We need to keep this guy around," Parker contributed.

"How did it go with those little blue roan colts?" Red inquired of Ben as they drove toward Raidy's Springs.

"Aw, Walt has them pretty gentle," Ben replied.

"You rattle a bucket of grain and they'll come a running! I going to hate turning them back to the wilds."

The sun was still hovering above the horizon when they reached Raidy's Springs. They had cached the quad and settled down in their hiding place. Parker immediately wrapped a blanket around him and closed his eyes for a nap.

Too restless to sit down, Ben was walking around, inspecting the gate panels. Suddenly, he came running back to the others!

"Horses coming," he exclaimed. "Pretty fast! Looks like a fair sized herd."

Fully alert now, the three wranglers awaited the arrival of the wild horses! Soon a dust cloud became a group of fast moving horses. Led by a black stallion with a prominent white star on its forehead, they passed the hidden watchers and entered the corral at a fast trot, headed for the Springs!

The three men sprinted for the gate panels and within seconds, had them snapped into place. Still undetected by the wild ones, Red and the others made their way back to the quad.

"Say, Red. I think Ben is bringing us good luck," Parker declared. "Let's go on over to the Willow Creek."

The half-moon gave off sufficient light, so they could travel without headlights as they approached Willow Creek. They parked a quarter mile away lest they frighten away any horses in the vicinity. They walked carefully, without conversation, as they neared the corral entranced. Ben stopped suddenly and held up his hand. The others looked at him curiously, as he stiffened; listening intently.

"Horses at the Creek," he whispered softly.

Without argument, Red and Parker followed him as Ben stole forward to the gate panels and carefully, they carried them into place for the second time that night!

"I can't believe it," Red exulted! "Two herds caught in one night and it's only ten o'clock!"

"I tell you, Ben is bringing us good luck," Parker reiterated!

"Well, Ben. I wouldn't have heard those horses, until it was too late to get the gates in place," Red agreed. "I definitely owe you one for that!"

Ben smiled to himself in the dark and broke out the sandwiches that he had prepared. The trio drove back to camp, munching ham and cheese on rye. A happy crew!

The rest of the week was consumed by hauling the culls into town. One of the stallions was quite old and joined the culls. The remainder of the two herds was retained at Raidy's Springs until sufficient good mares could be trapped.

Saturday morning, Red was seen washing his jeep. Shortly before noon, he grinned at his friends, as he drove away.

"See you Sunday evening!"

CHAPTER 12

First Date

"Good grief, Red! You're supposed to eat the baby back ribs, not wear them!" Irene leaned across the small table and dabbed at some barbecue sauce on Red's cheek.

"I've been eating camp cooking so long, I forgot what real food tastes like," Red defended himself and smiled back at Irene. She was a very satisfactory dinner partner. "Besides, I skipped lunch."

Amused at Red's capacity for ribs and long finished with her petite steak, Irene sat back and sipped at her wine, as he finally devoured the last bite.

"Tell me about yourself, Red. You haven't always been a ranger and chasing wild horses." Irene smiled across the table at him.

"Well, except for a tour in the army, that's about the only job I've had that amounted to anything," Red answered. He had a sip of wine before continuing. "I worked at a fast food place out of high school before joining up. I had two tours in Iraq. It was a very bad scene!" Red's face sobered as some pictures flashed before his eyes!

"Anyhow, I kicked around for a year or so after my time with the military was up," Red continued after a short pause. "I couldn't stand inside work. Then I heard that the Bureau was looking for men with some background in horses, and I had grown up around them, so I applied and got on with them." Red grinned. "How about you? Have you always been a preacher's daughter?"

Irene chuckled. "Well, I think so. At least, as long as I can remember! I spent a year just kicking back after high school. I, too, worked at a fast food place. Then I went to Wyoming State one year. I was dubious about attending college, where my dad taught, but I didn't like State, so I agreed to go to Crossroads on a trial basis and loved it. This is my second year and I hope to be a journalist, when I graduate."

"Meeting Miss Castell was a real boon! I need to thank you for that! We have met for lunch a couple times and seem to have hit it off. She is a big fan of yours," Irene added with just a twinge of jealousy.

It was a relatively short date, but their goodnight kiss reflected better things to come, and Irene invited Red to join her at church the following day!

Red retired to his motel room that night with a warm feeling!

CHAPTER 13

Supplying Horses

Red paused at his labor to look at the herd of wild horses, milling around at the far side of the corral at the Seeps. The three wranglers were building the small pen and loading area in preparation of moving the culls to town. It was the fourth herd they had trapped since his date with Irene.

The herd was a little unusual, as most of the mares were not good enough to keep, but too good to cull out. He was going to have a difficult time deciding, which way to go.

His cell phone rang at that moment. It was his boss, Richard Cooper.

"Good morning, Boss."

"Yes, good morning. Red, I am sending out a man, who says he needs a couple dozen wild horses for a rodeo. Will you talk to him and see, if we can help? That would be just some horses, we don't have to feed and take care of. I'll give you his phone number and you can effect a rendezvous. His name is William Whitehorse. I checked on Walt yesterday. He is still wearing the casts, but the doctors say, maybe in a couple more weeks."

"I will call him, Boss. And thanks for the update on Walt," Red replied.

They finished the loading corral in early afternoon

and returned to base camp. A bright red, dual wheeled pickup was waiting for them. It had a pair of large cow horns mounted on its hood, oversized tires and bright chrome wheel rims. A tall, slim, dark-faced man of Indian descent, stepped out of the truck, as they drove in.

"Howdy, I'm Bill Whitehorse," the man greeted Red with outstretched hand. "You would be Red."

"I'm Red," Red admitted. "What can I do for you?"

"Well, like I explained over the phone, I need a couple dozen wild horses. Don't need to be fancy, just strong, healthy stock. I run a rodeo exhibition, where we turn out six wild horses at a time on a halter rope, with three cowboys per horse. The first team that gets a saddle on the horse and rides it around the arena gets the purse. Every team that gets aboard and stays there gets to keep the horse. It's real popular with the cowboys, as it takes a lot more skill, than just sticking on a bronco's saddle." Bill Whitehorse explained.

"We have a new herd, trapped at the Seeps," Red suggested. "We got time before dark to drive over and look at them. You are welcome to stay over with us for supper and or for the night, if you like."

"Take you up on both," Whitehorse declared. "I got my sleeping bag in the back. Reckon we can take my rig. I got four wheel drive."

The two of them headed for the red pickup.

"Parker, can you guys stir up some grub, while we are gone?" Red called out over his shoulder.

"Most of these will work fine." Bill Whitehorse rubbed his hands in satisfaction. "Can't use the stud or those yearlings, but most of the rest will work great! Could you haul them into town, where I can pick them up with a semi?"

"I can do that," Red agreed. "There are none of these, including the stallion that I want to turn back on the range, so I will need to make two trips."

"How soon do you expect to have another herd trapped," Bill asked.

"It is hard to predict," Red replied. "It will take a minimum of two days to move these out. Then catching

---

79

another herd is iffy. Sometimes we trap one right away, and then, it might be several days before we catch another. We have three water holes fenced, but can only watch one at a time, as it takes two of us."

"Could you watch two water holes at a time, if I helped," Bill inquired.

"Why, yes," Red was surprised. "You and I could watch Raidy's Springs, while Ben and Parker check Willow Creek."

"I'm willing to help, where ever I can. I get the horses free, but I have to pay for boarding them, until I get them to Cheyenne," Bill declared. "If you don't mind feeding me, I'll stick around!"

Red explained Bill's role in the upcoming days to the others over supper.

"We will take a load in tomorrow and let them sort out, what Bill gets, and, what goes into the cull pasture," Red finished. "Day after tomorrow, I'll take the second load in, and we can watch the water holes that night. While I'm gone, you can ease some of the herd over toward Willow Creek and Raidy's Springs. Hopefully, we will have another herd in the next few days and can move the loading coral accordingly."

"Where and when is your next meet," Ben wanted to know. "Could I participate?"

"Sure. Don't see why not. There is a fifty dollar entrance fee. You need three guys and each needs to know their job," Bill answered. "I plan to be in Cheyenne next month. Cheyenne Frontier Days I always draws a good crowd."

William Whitehorse stayed for two weeks. The original two trailer loads went into town without mishap, but it took four herds to fill out his requirement for "not too fancy, but strong and healthy horses". Meantime, another choice stallion was trapped and held, until they had a small harem collected for him. He was being held at Raidy's Springs.

"Four or five more mares and we'll turn him out," Red remarked with satisfaction.

———

They had just unloaded four black yearlings, which they had removed from an old stallion, which had joined the culled herd. The men were leaning on the fence, admiring the new harem, which they had amassed.

"Boss, the horses are getting pretty well thinned out around the Seeps and Willow Creek," Ben mentioned. "Wolf Creek had a lot of horses, when I was coyote hunting up there last spring."

"Yeah, I been thinking that we need another pen. Unless we pull up the fencing from Willow and Seeps, I'll have to order some more panels," Red agreed.

"Might get more customers for Wolf Creek, if we close off Seeps and Willow Creek," Parker interjected.

"I know. I just am reluctant to spend more money on the fencing," Red replied.

"A mile of panels should give us another eighty acre pen," Parker argued. "We still have one mile on our list to your boss."

Red answered by flipping open his cell phone.

"Hello, this is Red Iverson. Give me Jeff with fencing. Hi, Jeff. How soon can you get me another mile of that aluminum panel fencing? Four days? Go ahead and order it. Call me when it gets in." Red signed off.

"I must say, you don't dink around, once you've made up your mind!" Parker stated with a grin.

"Boss, that rodeo is coming up soon, wonder if I could get a few days off to practice with my buddies," Ben asked.

"Don't see why not," Red responded. "Parker and I can build the fence around Wolf Creek, when the fencing gets here. We will stand watch at the Seeps a few more nights, and you can take off whenever you want."

"Hey! If we catch another herd, maybe Ben could practice with the real thing a few times. That should give him a leg up on the other contestants." Parker was excited.

"Great idea," Red enthused. "Ben, you round up your team and Parker and I will trap a herd; you pick out a good candidate to practice on, and win the race. It's a slam dunk!"

Ben grinned at Red's optimism. "Well, maybe not a slam dunk, but definitely an improvement on our odds!"

Fortune smiled on them in that the second night, a herd was trapped and several candidates for practicing for the Wild Horse Race was among them.

CHAPTER 14

Prepping For Wild Horse Racing

Trace was a burly, dark skinned Indian. His hands were scarred and calloused and his face showed signs of many encounters, with one ear slightly larger than the other one. Standing at six feet two inches, he looked well suited for his role on Ben's team!

Micah, the third man on Ben's team, was of lighter skin, showing his mixed bloodlines. He, too, was big, but lithe and quick on his feet. Ben had made a good selection of teammates!

The bay mare was more than a little frightened. She was in a small ten by ten foot pen with two ropes around her neck and held in opposite directions by Red and Parker, as Ben and Trace slid a halter on her head.

Red and Parker now released their ropes, and the mare was free in the pen except for the halter with a fifteen foot rope, which trailed on the ground. All was set!

Ben set his saddle carefully on the ground so it could be picked up quickly, about thirty feet from the pen, and the three men waited for Red's signal before rushing to the pen and through the gate that Parker opened for them!

The team gathered up the trailing rope with Micah closest to the horse and Ben at the furthest end as the mare burst from the pen! They clung to the rope, attempting to slow and stop the plunging mare, as Trace used his weight and great strength. Micah worked hand over hand toward the halter. The mare reared and plunged, trying to evade the men, until Micah got close enough to her head to grab the halter. He then wrapped his arms around the mare's head, using the combined weight of Trace and Micah to stop her plunging, while Ben gathered up his saddle to toss on the plunging horse.

With both Trace and Micah holding down the mare's head, Ben was able to cinch the saddle tight and climb aboard! Ben yelled, and the horse was released to buck and run, while Ben fought to remain in the saddle and steer the mare along the fence line of the Seeps corral! Red stood by on his saddle horse, in case he was needed.

Using his spurs and hauling her head up with the halter to convince the mare to stop bucking and run, Ben whooped as she finally broke into a gallop, following the fence. Ben circled the bay back to the starting point and slid off. His face was wreathed with a broad grin.

"Congratulation! You won first prize, a bay mare." Red chuckled as he, too, swung down from his horse.

"Good ride," Micah chipped in.

"A good performance, all around," Parker added.

"Seriously, you can keep the bay mare, if you want her," Red told Ben. "She ain't a bad one. Better than our usual cull."

"Sure, I'll keep her and much obliged," Ben replied. "I would like to try that black, now, if my team is good for another go."

"Sure, Ben. I barely worked up a sweat." Trace grinned through his dust covered face.

"I'm game. Trace did all the work on the bay," Micah agreed.

Parker and Red mounted their respective saddle horses to crowd the sturdy black mare into the small pen from the corral as Ben and Micah unsaddled and released the bay mare in to the large pen, surrounding the Seeps.

Saddling the black went even smoother than the bay, except Ben was unable to get the black mare's head up, and she continued to buck for an extended time, before giving up

84

and running down the fence line. Ben was exhausted, when he leaped off!

"Hey! That looked more like the bronc riding event than a horse race, Ben," Trace chuckled, as he and Micah took the horse from Ben.

"I think I have had enough fun for the day," Ben panted as he leaned against the fence! "I couldn't pull her head up. Once she got it between her knees, I didn't have the strength to pull it up!"

"Maybe if you took a turn around the horn with the halter rope, before Trace releases her head," Red suggested. "You could whip it off, when she starts to run."

"That might work," Parker added. "If she can't get her head down, she can't buck. Probably rear though!"

"I'll try that tomorrow," Ben replied.

"Parker, you and I will stand watch at Wolf Creek again, tonight," Red instructed. "Ben, you and your gang are on your own."

"Red, could I have that black mare? Since she is half broke already," Micah asked. "I could play with her this afternoon."

"Be my guest, Micah," Red replied. "The black is yours."

Red and Parker were back in camp before midnight, having caught a herd during the early evening hours.

"Big pinto stud leading this bunch," Red mentioned, the next morning at breakfast. "We already have a good stallion at Raidy's Springs, so we have to haul one of them off. Might be that he is big enough to carry your frame, Trace. If you can ride him, of course!" Red grinned slyly at the big man across from him.

"A pinto, you say?" Trace's face lit up. "I could always get Ben to take the edge off him, first."

Red's reply was cut off by the ringing of his cell phone. It was his boss, Richard Cooper.

"Red, when are you coming into town again," he asked after a brief greeting.

"We caught a bunch last night, Boss. We will get the loading pen up today and bring a load of culls in tomorrow, if we are lucky on loading them," Red replied.

"Good! You need to meet me for lunch at the hotel at one o'clock. Be prompt. If the loading takes too long, drive in ahead of it, and let Parker bring the load of horses. I am meeting someone that wants to talk with you." Cooper said goodbye and hung up.

"What was that about," Parker inquired as Red slid his cell phone back into his pocket.

Red repeated the conversation and got to his feet. "Reckon we better get moving, get to bed early and breakfast by candlelight again, tomorrow."

"We would like to help," Micah declared. "We got another week to practice."

"You're on." Red waved them toward the truck. "Parker, bring a quad over, when you finished with the kitchen chores. Fix us some lunch to bring along, would you, please?"

Parker nodded his head and started gathering up the dishes.

Trace grinned with delight, as they drove the wild bunch into the loading corral. The black, red and white pinto stallion shone against the rising sun. Just a bit heavy for a fast saddle horse, he was still surprisingly light on his feet. A fitting match for the big Indian, who was to own him!

They had finished the corral early the day before, due to the added help from Ben's team. The added men on horseback, also sped up the culling out and loading, and Red was on his way in good time to make his luncheon appointment.

"Don't you ride that pinto before I get back, so I can watch," he warned Trace as he climbed into the truck cab.

"Okay, Red. We will try to get a halter on him and that's all," replied Trace.

Red was surprised to see his boss with a stranger, waiting for him at the corrals. He had phoned ahead that he was on his way to reassure his boss that he would be on time. Richard Cooper introduced the stranger as J.B. Honeycutt, but nothing was said as to why he was here, or why he wanted to talk to Red.

Finally, after Red pushed back his chair after an ample lunch, J.B Honeycutt cleared his throat! The talking part was to begin.

"Mister Iverson, could you briefly explain your program and your reasoning behind your plan?"

"Please call me, Red." Red proceeded to explain what he was doing and why, adding his plan for the future.

"How many head of wild horses have you trapped and brought in, Red?"

"About two hundred fifty," Red replied.

"Actually, two fifty-three," Cooper put in, consulting his notebook. "And turned back on the range, sixty seven mares and yearlings and four studs."

"Do you have any pictures of the ones that you turned back on the range," was J.B.'s next question.

"Sure do!" Red whipped out his cell phone and after a few taps handed it across the table. "This was the stallion on the first herd, we trapped. The next one is one of his three yearlings that I turned out with a bay stud, later on."

"Whew!" J.B. whistled. "You turned a stud like that back into the wilds?"

"It's the only way we can improve the wild herds is to cull out the poor ones and leave the choice," Red argued. "In a few years, the public will be fighting over the horses, we cull out. We just need to stay ahead of the inbreeding!"

J.B. continued to thumb through Red's photos.

"Richard, these are choice animals. I'm beginning to see what this young man has sold you on. The Adobe horse herd will be the envy of the whole Bureau!"

"On top of that, Red and his crew have been working only six months and he has culled almost a quarter of our over stock," Richard Cooper declared. "And, he is under budget!"

J.B. handed the cell phone back to Red.

"I am really impressed with, what you are doing, Red. It is difficult to imagine anyone opposing your program, but the fact is; there is some serious opposition out there. Some animal lover groups are spreading lies that we are killing off the culls, which you are bring in. Another rumor is that you

87

are selling the choice animals and pocketing the money. Teresa Castell has been a big help with her articles in disclaiming many of the rumors, but they still exist!"

"But why would anyone be against our program," Red protested.

"Unfortunately, just because it is a good thing, doesn't follow that everybody will be for it, Red," Richard Cooper stated.

"You have an ardent supporter in William Whitehorse, Red," J.B. continued. "He has many influential friends. However, his support has brought your work to the attention of some of the wrong people. One of them is Rick Stonewood. Rick owns a company called Drovers Inc. He covers all the states that contain wild horse herds and for a fee will make a big drive, using helicopters, dirt bikes and quads to sweep the area clean of wild horses."

"Rick has a good thing going and no competition, and he likes it that way. If your system spreads, and I think it will, he will be out of business."

"I am in charge of the Lander Field Office, which administers to the Conant Creek/Muskrat Basin area and would like to copy your program, maybe hire one of your helpers that knows the ropes. There is one problem. My bosses are sold on Drovers Inc. and are aiming for a late winter drive. I don't think I can stop that."

"Actually, you could work with that, Mister Honeycutt," Red replied. "You need to hire a bunch of savvy horse wranglers to separate the good stock out and turn them back out. Separate all the culls out, regardless of how many there are and keep them away from your good studs. Then, all you need to do is maintain the herds and control the inbreeding."

"Yes, that occurred to me, but the cost of the big drive drains my budget and I can't afford a crew like yours," J. B. answered.

Red tossed up his hands. "Well, it would be at least two years before you would need to cull out the yearlings."

J.B. shook his head. "Could you email me some of your pictures? I'd like to show them to my bosses."

"Sure. I have dozens of pictures." Red dug out his

---

phone again. "Here is a couple of the blue roan with his new harem!"

"Oh my! Wouldn't it be great to own a horse herd like those," J.B. enthused. "Think of the colts, those mares will turn out!"

As the three men rose from the table to leave, J.B. again turned to Red.

"I should warn you again about Rick Stonewood! He is rumored to have eliminated competition in unorthodox methods," J.B. looked troubled. "He is a dangerous man and isn't above breaking the law to gain his desires!"

Red answered his cell phone, as he drove back toward the base camp. It was Richard Cooper.

"Red, I just wanted to tell you to heed J.B.s warnings! Rick Stonewood is a bad character, and you need to look out for yourself!"

"I'll do the best I can, Boss," Red assured him.

CHAPTER 15

Stonewood

Ben was standing making pancakes and Trace and Micah were devouring them like potato chips. Finally, he called a halt.

"I got two more, and they are mine," he declared. "You two would just keep eating pancakes until noon and then want lunch!"

Micah ignored him and stuffed the last of his pancake in his mouth.

"What did the big boss have on his mind," he directed at Red between chewing.

Red poured himself a last cup of coffee before answering.

"Apparently, the main reason of the meeting was to meet J.B. Honeycutt, who heads the Wind River section of the Bureau. He wanted to know, how I ran our operation."

Red went on to relate the gist of the conversation at lunch. He went interrupted, until he mention the name of Rick Stonewood.

Ben stopped his forkful of pancake halfway to his mouth.

"Rick Stonewood," he yelped. "I've heard a lot about him! None of it good! A local fellow, over in Montana out bid him on a government wild horse drive. Only thing, that fellow had an accident with his helicopter and was killed, so

Stonewood got the contract by default. Every time someone tries to compete against Stonewood, something happens. Guy in Nevada. His kid disappeared from High School for a week. He took his family and left the country. Stonewood is bad news!"

Red looked startled. "Wow, I had no idea, he was that desperate. Surely, we aren't that big a threat to his business! There must be a couple dozen areas that the Bureau controls. We aren't trying to compete with him."

"I don't know, Red. I've heard stories, too," Micah inserted.

"Well, we can't just sit here shaking in our boots," Red stated. "We have work to do. We need to get those mares from Wolf Creek over to Raidy's Springs and do something with that pinto stud. In addition, we have two more mares for you to practice on, Ben. We need a plan!"

"I have an idea, Red. Why don't we practice on the pinto stud! That way we kill two birds with one stone," Ben advanced. "After I ride him once, we can bring him and the black mare over here and Trace and Micah can work with them. Then, we can take the good mares over to the stud at Raidy's Springs. That will open up Wolf Creek for another catch."

"Good idea, Ben," Red agreed. "I want to fence Mustang Wells next. Let's figure on getting that done, and then just relaxing, and concentrating on the Cheyenne Frontier Days. That sorrel at Raidy's Springs will have to wait to get the rest of his harem!"

The saddle horses were quickly loaded in the trailer and they were on their way to Wolf Creek. The pinto stallion proved to be a dud. With two ropes on him, he became gentle as a lamb.

"Red, this was a runaway," Trace discovered. "He has a brand on him. So much for practice, Ben."

"That doesn't make me mad," Ben chuckled. "Throw your saddle on him and see how he reacts."

With Trace in the saddle, the pinto stud gave a few crow hops, but seemed almost eager to oblige and raised his tail and head proudly, ready to perform. Trace trotted him around the corral, halted the stud in front of the watchers, and swung down.

"He was a tough one, but I mastered him," Trace grinned.

"And I let you have him for free," Red pretended regret.

"How about a little help here," Parker had a rope on another bay mare and was trying to get a halter on her.

Micah and Red rushed to his aid, and soon Ben's team were in action again.

The culls were loaded and carried to town, and the mares that were earmarked to turn back on the range, were hauled to Raidy's Springs.

It was time for the Cheyenne Frontier Days!

CHAPTER 16

The Rodeo

Walt was still wearing an arm in a sling, but was well enough to enjoy the rodeo. He was accompanied by Teresa Castell, his sister, Beth, Red, Parker and Irene Fallon.

Red had been driving to Laramie every weekend to see Irene, frequently with Walt, who was dating Teresa.

They had just finished watching the Women's Barrel Race, which was won by an attractive brunette, Marlene Fletcher, on a black Morgan horse. Miss Fletcher was wearing a black riding habit with white shirt, set off by red fringe on sleeves and yoke. Jet-black boots and a white Stetson hat complimented the four white stocking feet and blaze face of the Morgan. They made a striking combination.

The arena was being cleared for the Calf Roping event, followed by Bull Riding. Bronc Riding would be the following day with Wild Horse Racing, one of the big attractions, at the very last.

It was the third day of the annual Cheyenne Frontier Days Rodeo. Although they were enjoying the rodeo events, Red and Parker were not used to inactivity and were getting a little restless

"Let's look up Ben and see if he needs anything," Parker whispered to Red, accompanied by a nudge in the ribs.

"Parker and I need to stretch our legs," Red relayed to Irene. "We won't be long."

The two wranglers rose to their feet and headed down toward the work area. After a lengthy search, they located Ben and his team.

"Hey, guys. Anything we can do to help you get ready," Red asked of Ben.

"As a matter of fact, yes," Ben replied. "Would you take Trace and buy him a soda and or a hamburger or a milkshake or anything to get him away for an hour or so! He is driving us nuts!"

"We can do that," Red laughed and taking Trace's arm, they left for the snack bar. Red was leading the group as they stood in line for their turn to order. He ordered a beer each for himself and Parker, and two double cheeseburgers and a large power drink for Trace. He paid with a credit card and then reached for the beer.

A burly hand grabbed Red's wrist and a harsh voice rang out.

"That's my beer!"

Red looked around to see a large, dark faced Indian hovering over him.

"I think you are mistaken, my friend," Red replied. "I just paid for them, ask the proprietor."

"I'm not your friend and I don't give a s---- what the proprietor says! I am taking that beer," the man ripped out.

"Well, now, maybe you should rethink this." Trace stepped up to face the stranger. He reached over and grabbed the exposed thumb of the hand gripping Red's wrist. Trace twisted the thumb backward, and the stranger began to howl.

"Turn loose of me, you bastard! I was only funnin!"

"Yeah! Right!" Trace still held the thumb. "Maybe someone sent you to rough Red up! Who?"

"I can't say except, I'm supposed to tell him to find a new job, if he wants to stay healthy," the big Indian got out. "I don't know who sent me! Honest!"

"Let him go, Trace," Red interrupted. "I can guess who sent him. Pick up your burgers and drink, and let's go."

"You think, this was a message from Rick Stonewood," Trace asked, as they made their way back to

Ben and Micah.

"From what I have heard about him, I'd bet on it," Red replied.

"You're going to have to keep Trace around for a body guard," Ben remarked, when they had related the incident!

"Well, I am going to start carrying my little thirty-eight pistol. As a ranger, I am allowed. The trick is to see trouble coming." Red shook his head.

"We better get back to the others," Parker remarked, "or they will send Walt to look for us!"

"Better we don't say anything to the girls about this," Red mentioned. "I don't want them worrying about me!"

The others agreed.

The Calf Roping event was just starting when Red and Parker regained their seats.

"How is Ben's team doing," inquired Walt.

"They're doing fine, I think," Red laughed. We had to escort Trace to the snack bar to soothe his restless spirit with a couple cheeseburgers!"

That drew a chuckle of understanding.

"These boys are recording some pretty fast times. There are no amateurs here," Walt remarked as the cowboy in the arena stood up with his calf securely tied.

"Let's stroll through Frontier Town," Teresa suggested after the final Bronc Riding event.

"Good idea," Parker agreed. "We can catch supper at the Buckin Bar and maybe dance a bit."

"We should swing by and pick up Ben and the boys," Red said. "It's been almost two hours since Trace's last feeding! He's probably starved!"

The group laughed and stood up, following the crowd to the exit.

The teams stood restlessly in front of their respective gates, where their wild horses were being prepared, their saddles sat nearby. The Wild Horse Race was about to begin!

The warning whistle sounded, all was ready and the

six teams rushed for the gates as the bell rang, the crowd roared as six horses burst from their pens. Immediately, chaos reigned! Several of the plunging, rearing and kicking horses came through the gates with three cowboys clinging to the long halter rope. One was towing a lone cowboy, lying on his stomach, at full speed.

"That one is gone," Walt laughed and indeed the lone cowboy released the rope and rolled to a stop!

"There's Ben," squealed Beth. "Oh, they are much better than the rest!"

Indeed they were. The practice drills were paying off as Micah went swiftly hand over hand up the rope of the plunging black mustang as the mustang made little progress, when anchored by Trace and Ben.

As Micah got a hold of the halter, he threw an arm over the horse's head, using all his weight to keep the mare from rearing and gave a yell. Trace responded by joining him and adding his weight to control the horse as Ben raced for his saddle. In minutes, Ben had the saddle on, cinched, and leaped aboard.

Micah and Trace released the mustang's head and she attempted to buck, but Ben had hitched the halter rope around the saddle horn and the black mare quickly gave up trying to get her head down and commenced to run.

Well ahead of the other contestants, Ben and the black mare raced by them and circled the arena to the sounds of the cheering of the crowd. Two other contestants had gotten aboard their mustangs, one mustang was running wildly with a saddle on its back and two more were running free with only the halter rope trailing them.

"Ladies and gentlemen," the announcer called out on his speaker system, "Ben Wiley and his team have won first place in this heat, but don't go away. We have two more heats. Just a bit of trivia. Ben and his team has turned in the fastest time for the Wild Horse Race since its inception! How about that?"

The crowd roared its approval! Ben Wiley had suddenly become a favorite!

Red and the group stayed for the other two heats of the Wild Horse Race, but all were confident that Ben, Trace

---

96

and Micah had the trophy in the bag! Indeed, Ben had, by a large margin!

The next day was Sunday and the entire group attended Cowboy Church. A well-known western band provided the music and the minister removed his Stetson to deliver the sermon.

He read from Genesis, where God made heaven and earth and all the living things. He stressed how The Lord made Man dominion over them.

"It is not the policy of rodeos to mistreat God's creatures, primarily horses and cattle. We do pit man against animal to the detriment of both sides, at times," the minister stated.

This drew a chuckle from the sanctuary!

"We need to practice personal care of our animal friends, but not to stop there. We need to do our best to prevent our government and other organizations from mistreating our commission of caring for the animal kingdom. I am particularly interested in following treatment of wild horses in the state of Wyoming and more interested in the area around Adobe Town."

"Many of the general public are of the opinion that the wild horses should be left alone to fend for themselves and man slash government should be "hands off" regarding controlling them. I am not in agreement with this theory. The horse is not basically a wild animal, but a domestic animal released to the wild, and God did not create an enemy to control their growth and expansion. The wild horse has no natural enemies except man, himself."

"Left to itself, the wild horse will double in population, every few years and inbreeding will deteriorate the quality of the animal and as grass becomes scarce, many will starve and freeze to death during the winter. Does that sound like 'taking dominion over God's creatures'?"

"I realize this is not a typical Sunday sermon, but as a spokesman for The Lord, I feel it my duty to point out some of these facts! We have in the congregation today a young man, who is revolutionizing the way the government handles this problem. He is in charge of the horse herds in the Adobe Town area of Wyoming. I am hoping I can persuade Red

---

97

Iverson to explain his operation, and the results he hopes to obtain!"

"Red, would you come forward and speak to us?"

Red sat in his pew, dumbfounded! He had no warning anything like this would occur! An elbow jab from Irene, who sat beside him, brought him out of his trance.

"Red, this your chance to set a lot of people's mind straight," Irene whispered. "Just go tell them like it is!"

"Why, uh, I, yes." Red floundered for words, as he struggled to his feet and walked to the front on the church.

"Just tell us, what you have been doing and why, Red," the pastor encouraged.

Slowly recovering, Red began to speak. He explained how there were twice as many wild horses on the range than the grass would support, and how he and his men were trapping them a herd at a time, saving the best mares and matching them with good quality stallions and taking the rest to Rawlings.

"They are poor quality mares, but they are taken to private ranches and cared for, while we search for a permanent home for them. Many are halter broke and sold for small amounts to the public. A young boy doesn't need a pure bred Arabian to learn too ride and love." Red grew more at ease as he talked. "We sell dozens some months."

"As an added incentive, the herds, that we have left, are of high quality, and their offspring will be very desirable to the more selective buyers."

A hand was raised in the audience. "Where can we go to purchase these animals?"

"Just contact the Bureau of Land Management, and they can point you to a number of sites, here in Wyoming and other States," Red replied.

"Thank you, Red. Both for your words and for the hard work, which you are doing to preserve these magnificent creatures," the pastor said , as Red returned to his seat.

CHAPTER 17

The Warning

Red returned to wild horse hunting with mixed emotions. It was good to get back to some meaningful activity, but he was going to miss the sweet presence of Irene Fallon!

Red called Mister Cooper and related the confrontation at the snack bar.

"I am concerned, Red. You must take every precaution! Keep those two men with you. I will put them on another payroll account and call it security. Be a good idea to pick up a couple of good rifles, when you get a chance. Be sure Walt knows about this."

"You mean that I am not the only target, Boss," Red exclaimed.

"I don't know, Red. Stonewood is very unpredictable." Richard Cooper sounded worried.

The windshield shattered in a thousand pieces, simultaneously with the thud of the bullet imbedding in the seat beside them!

They had caught another herd of wild horses in Wolf Creek the night before, and were returning from erecting the loading pen in preparation to the usual culling of the herd.

Red braked sharply and leaped from the driver's seat.

Crouched by the front tire, his eyes searched the terrain before him. His pistol was gripped tightly in his right hand.

There was no sound except for the heavy breathing of his and Parker's, who had exited the other side of the truck at the same time.

"Anybody hurt in the back seat," Red inquired in a low voice.

"We are okay, Red," came the muffled voice from the back. The three men were huddled down, trying to hide behind the back of the front seat.

After a few minutes, Red stood up. "I guess that was just another warning, or he would be still shooting. We can't sit here all night!" He got back in the truck. "Call the sheriff's department, Parker, and report this."

Red started up the truck, drove a little way off the trail, and stopped again.

"Ben, there is a small whisk broom under my seat. See if you can reach it. Maybe you can get this broken glass swept out of here."

Red slipped out his cell phone and got out of the truck again.

"Hi, Boss. I think I just got a second warning from our friend, Stonewood. Yeah, somebody shot out our windshield, while we were returning from Wolf Creek. Just now. Ben is sweeping out the glass and, Parker is talking to the Sheriff Department now. We will just go ahead as usual, load up some culls and bring them in tomorrow. I can maybe get the windshield fixed then. Don't know, what else I can do, Boss. I am not going to run! You might get me an old army tank to drive around in. Sorry, Boss, excuse my joke! Yes, Sir. I will see you tomorrow." Red replaced his phone

"Mister Cooper didn't appreciate your levity, I take it," Parker was grinning.

Red made a face, but said nothing.

"It's as clean as I can get it without a vacuum, Red," Ben declared

Everybody got back in the vehicle, and they drove on to camp.

Red's cell phone beeped as he was getting out of the

truck. It was Walt.

"Red, I just got a call from Teresa. She was hysterical! She went to pick up her mail and there was a snake in her mailbox. I am about to drive up to see her."

"A snake in her mailbox?" Red was thunderstruck initially, but then it dawned on him! "Rick Stonewood!"

"What did you say? Rick Stonewood, that crook. What has he to do with us," Walt exclaimed.

"Sorry, Walt. I should have told you sooner, but I didn't think about his bothering my friends! I got a warning in Cheyenne to quit my job, and then today somebody shot out our windshield. We think Stonewood resents our success with the wild horse herds and sees us as a threat to his mass drives." Red apologized.

"Damn! That SOB saw us together at the rodeo and will get at you through your friends, since he can't scare you," Walt raged. "Beth! I got to warn Beth!" Walt hung up abruptly!

Red feverishly punched Irene's phone number.

"Irene! Are you all right?"

"Red. Strange you should call. I'm still at school. I went out to drive home and all four of my tires were flat! The AAA came out, but said they had been stuck with a sharp knife. Why would anyone deliberately ruin all my tires?"

"Oh, Darling, I am sorry! Somebody is attacking me through my friends!" Red tore his hair in frustration. "Don't go home! When you get your tires fixed, drive over to Teresa's. I will get somebody to watch over you, until this is settled!"

"But, Red, I can't just--. Irene interrupted herself. "Red, how about you? You must be in danger! Oh, you must be careful! If something happened to you---."

"Don't worry, Darling. I'll be all right. Just do what I asked," Red reassured her.

Red again dialed his boss. There was no levity in his voice, as he pleaded for help!

"Boss, they are going after my friends! Somebody knifed all of Irene Fallon's car tires while she was parked at the college and Teresa Castell found a snake in her mailbox.

101

I sent Irene over to Teresa' place. Could you get a couple of security people over there to look after them? Thanks, Boss. Walt is checking on his sister now."

Walt let his SUV glide quietly to a stop behind the grey sedan, parked across the street from, where his sister, Beth worked. He checked his heavy pistol before sliding out of his vehicle. A man was sitting behind the steering wheel of the sedan, reading a magazine, the window down to let out the smoke from the cigarette, smoldering in the ashtray.

The man froze at the sound of a cocking pistol, and the barrel dug into his left ear.

"Just keep both hands locked tightly on that sex book, Roscoe, if you want to keep those few brains that you have in your head."

With his left hand, Walt reached in and removed the keys from the ignition. With the same hand, he opened the car door.

"Now get out slowly, keeping that magazine opened tight with both hands, and walk to the rear of the car." Walt stepped back, bringing the door with him, but holding the revolver steady.

"You still working for that crumb, Stonewood, Roscoe?" Walt's grim face and icy eyes belied the lightness of his tone of voice.

"Don't know what you're talkin about," Roscoe muttered.

Walt's searching fingers found the key hole to the trunk, and he raised it full open.

"Get in!"

"You can't do this! I wasn't doin nothin!" Roscoe was whining, now!

"Shut up!" Walt's voice was cold and menacing. "You are going in there alive or dead! Your choice!" He raised the pistol to eye level, aimed just above Roscoe's nose.

Roscoe quickly jumped into the trunk and Walt gently closed the lid.

"If I hear any noise from there, I am going to fire a couple rounds through the lid," Walt stated as he strode swiftly across the street to his sister's office.

He passed Beth's little Honda and noticed the front door to her office was ajar. He pushed it gently open.

Beth was the last to leave the office, but as she turned back to key the deadbolt on the front door, a heavy hand clutched her shoulder and a second one reached past her and reopened the door. She was thrust back into the office.

"What do you want," she demanded angrily, as she turned to face her attacker. "Get out of here!"

"Oh Ho! Aren't you the spunky one! My orders are just to slap you around a bit, but a cute bit of fluff like you, why it's a waste not to have a bit of fun," the stocky attacker laughed.

Beth shook loose from his grasp and tried to run around him to get to the door, but he grabbed her around the waist with one arm and ripped at her blouse with the other.

"You dirty--." Beth still had the door keys in her hand. She raked them down her attacker' face, aiming at his eyes!

"You little bitch! I'll teach you." He cocked a fist and smashed her in the face, stunning her. She fell backward on the carpet.

The man fell on her, tearing at her denim trousers.

"Damn these Levi's," he muttered.

He didn't hear the door being pushed open, nor the footsteps across the floor. Neither did he feel the heavy pistol, when it crashed down on the back of his head! Not until later!

Walt picked up his little sister, carried her out to her car, and laid her on the front seat. Then he called the police.

Walt ran quickly to a hose bib, next to the building and wet his bandana. Returning to the car, he washed Beth's face until she stirred. A large dark swelling appeared on her cheek where she had been struck. Her eyes reflected the horror that she felt, but when she recognized her brother, she commenced to sob.

There wasn't room in Richard Cooper's office so they met in the conference room.

Richard Cooper was speaking. "I can only express a

deep regret for, what has happened the last few days. I, in no way, expected a reaction such as this to the successful operation that you have accomplished, Mister Iverson."

He was speaking to Red's expanded crew of Parker, Ben, Trace, Micah and Walt.

"The sheriff found a picture of some of you on the rodeo stands."

"Like six blackbirds on a telephone line," Parker interjected.

"He found a copy on the two hoods that were involved in Miss Wiley's attack." Cooper glared at Parker for the interruption. "ACME Protection Agency has assigned two men to each of the ladies and two more on stand-by twenty four hours a day."

"Back to Miss Wiley's attack. The driver of the car, a Roscoe Billings, disclaims any connection to the man, Walt found physically attacking Miss Wiley. And his attorney is talking of a lawsuit against Walt for assault! The attacker, Ron Bauer, has no knowledge of Rick Stonewood and claims he was just passing by when Miss Wiley called to him and invited him in!"

"That's a damn lie," Walt jumped up angrily. "She was unconscious, when I came in. And how about that lump on her face? Does that look like she invited him to attack her?"

"I know, Walt," Richard Cooper soothed him. "The lawyers have to come up with some defense. Bauer won't get away with this! They are requesting bail, but it has been hinted to Bauer that his life might be at risk, if he is released. He has decided to stay in jail and just wait for the trial. Miss Wiley apparently did a job on Bauer's face," he added with satisfaction. "Needed seventeen stitches to close it!"

"He wouldn't get ten miles out of town. before he would have a fatal accident," Parker declared, undeterred by the frown from Richard Cooper.

"At any rate, gentlemen, I wanted to bring you up to date and to assure you that if any, or all of you wish to opt out of the program, I will understand and will write a favorable letter to your next employer," Richard Cooper finished.

"Not me. I'll not quit! Furthermore, I would like to figure a way to put a crimp in that SOB's tail." Red stood up. His red hair practically bristling! "I would like a favor, Boss. We don't have Internet out at camp. Would you look up everything you can find about Rick Stonewood? Where he was born. His parents, are they alive, does he have children. Where are they? Get every bit of scrap of information about him that is possible! I am looking for a weak link, a spot where he is vulnerable!"

"Be glad to do that for you, Red," Richard Cooper agreed. "I do need to make clear that we do not over step the boundaries of Christian principles, and/or legal boundaries!"

"You have my word, Boss," Red replied.

"I'm with Red all the way, Mister Cooper, and none of us will let you down," Parker declared with several nods of agreements from the others.

"We still have a corral full of wild horses to take care of, Red," Ben reminded them.

"You are right, Ben. And a broken windshield to get fixed," Red acknowledged.

"Anything I can do to ease your work, let me know." Richard Cooper stood up. The meeting was over.

"How is Beth doing," Red inquired of Walt as they walked from the conference room.

"Not real good, Red," Walt replied. "Even though that gorilla didn't have a chance to touch her, she is still filled with trauma. She doesn't even trust the guards, now. I would like to go with you, even though I can't ride yet, but Beth needs me beside her for now. She is taking off a week or so of sick leave. I wonder, if she could spend some time with Irene. They hit it off pretty well. What do you think?"

"Call her," Red urged. "And get her to call Beth. Beth could benefit from some Christian counseling."

With the windshield replaced on their truck, Red, with his crew increased to five, went back to wild horse trapping. With one difference! Either Red or Parker, who were excellent rifle shots from their military training, always had a high-powered rifle in their hands at all times.

Word came down from Richard Cooper that the wild horse round-up in the Wind River area was going forward with Drover's Inc. making the drive, and that Red and his crew was expected to take charge of culling the big herd, when the time came. Cooper was in the process of locating two dozen experienced horse wranglers to assist. Red and his crew were encouraged to submit any acquaintance that qualified.

Red was also requested to submit a list of requirements regarding corrals.

Red's list: two large cutting pens, three smaller holding pens, two small loading pens with ramps and at least two large semi-trailers for hauling the culls.

CHAPTER 18

Red Finds the Son

Ricky Stonewood was adopted by an English couple, Jeb and Marsha Stonewood and taken to Chicago to live. An extremely intelligent boy with a high IQ, he rebelled under the slightest discipline. Consequently, his school life was filled with detention and harsh lectures.

Several attempts at running away from home were somewhat successful, in that, he disappeared for two weeks at the age of thirteen. He was found by the police in the slum area, stealing food from an outdoor market.

His adoptive parents gave up at that point, and he was placed in the Home for Wayward Youth! Here he discovered some leadership abilities, leading a mass breakout at the age of seventeen.

Released into society on his eighteenth birthday, his rebellious activities continued, only with the knowledge that the adult penalties were a lot harsher, should he be caught! Charged with many misdeeds, he always avoided conviction, and he finally wisely decided to leave the Chicago area and moved west.

In Kansas City, he was hired by the Security Guardians and spent his evenings on guard duty. Here he married a teenager, Meg Harris, and she was immediately disowned by her family, who recognized Rick for what he was; a grown up juvenile delinquent! When the things he was guarding began disappearing, he was dismissed. He abandoned his bride and six-month-old son and moved again!

Still with no criminal record, he was able to get work with the Bureau of Land Management in Arizona. He participated in a government directed wild horse round-up, driving a quad and had a blast. Rick Stonewood had finally found work that he enjoyed! Somehow acquiring a large sum of money, he started up a company. He was able to convince some of the brass at BLM that he could conduct the wild horse drives cheaper and more efficiently than the BLM could and he was in business.

Anyone competing against him, would suddenly find hard luck pursuing them, and they would be forced to withdraw. Many rumors flourished, but no one ever brought charges against him, and Rick Stonewood continued to prosper!

Meanwhile, his abandoned wife, Meg, found work, doing menial household jobs, as she didn't even have a high school education. She divorced Rick and changed her name and her son's to Harris. She had called him, George, after her grandfather, who still claimed her as his granddaughter. When George was a junior in high school, she began receiving money from an anonymous source with the assurance that it would keep coming, provided George attended Princeton and became a lawyer.

Meg had never told George anything about his father, or about the mysterious money! When he questioned his mother, she evaded any reference to his father and indicated that her grandfather was helping with his schooling expenses.

The folder, which Red was reading, contained the same information as above except in much more stilted language. He closed the folder and thought for a minute.

"Stonewood apparently mellowed or something happened to make him look up his son and provide him with a first class education," Red mused. "I wonder if I should look him up."

Red made a call to Richard Cooper.

"Boss, I was looking at Stonewood's dossier and I would like to meet his son. Do I have some vacation time coming?"

"What do you have in mind, Red," Cooper asked.

"I don't really know, Boss. I just got a feeling Stonewood wouldn't like it. Maybe there is something I can use to defend myself!" Red was pretty unsure himself, and why he thought it was important!

"I'll think of some reason to send you there, so you won't be out a plane ticket or vacation time. You be careful. Stonewood could be keeping tabs on you. I'll call you with ticket info." Cooper hung up!

The young man, who Red had been following, turned into the entrance to the Student Lounge.

"At last," Red muttered to himself, as he had been trying to catch George Harris in a casual atmosphere for two days.

He got in line behind the young man and paid for coffee and a glazed donut.

"Care if I join you," Red asked as he set his coffee cup down across from young Harris.

Red had always found it easy to meet new friends and George Harris was no exception.

"Sure, sit down," he replied. "You look pretty suntanned to be a student. I'm George Harris, attorney in hopes," he chuckled as he extended his hand. "Haven't seen you around before."

"Red Iverson." Red extended his own hand to meet George's. "No, I'm no student. I am from back west where the sun shines. I am just visiting my girlfriend, who is taking a couple classes. She works for an attorney around here somewhere. I got some time to kill. How is the school treating you?"

"Great school," George Harris enthused. "I'm in my third year. Really good professors! I am in the top ten percent of my classes!"

"Hey, that's pretty good," Red applauded. "I understand Law is a tough course. You got family here."

"No, not here. Just my mom, back in Kansas City." George's face darkened. "I need to do well, so I can get on with a good law firm. My mom has about ruined her health, working two jobs to support us. I must move her to a warmer climate and reduce her workload. That takes money!"

"I am sorry," Red said sincerely. "Single parent, I assume." After George's nod, "It is tough for a woman to support a family alone. There are student loans available."

"Mom wouldn't hear of that! She says the burden of paying back a student loan is intolerable! My grandpa is helping out, but he isn't that well off either."

George got up to replenish his coffee.

"What do you do, out West where the sun shines?" George grinned, when he returned.

Red chuckled. "I work for the Bureau of Land Management in Wyoming. I'm in charge of managing the wild horse herds in one area there."

George paused in the act of sipping his coffee. "Wild horse herds? I didn't know we had any wild horses in this country. Why don't you just catch them and sell them to people that ride horses? Wouldn't that put you out of a job?"

Red chuckled again. "Not that simple! There are those who look at the horse herds as a national heritage, you know, like the grey wolf and or wild eagles, and that they need to be protected."

Red had George's interest now.

"So what exactly do you do to manage the herds?"

Red looked at his watch. He did not want to get into a discussion about his work.

"I need to take care of a few things, before I pick up Irene. Will you be here tomorrow? I enjoy chatting with you."

"Why sure, Red," George replied. "I'll save a table for you and see you tomorrow this same time."

Red went back to his rental car and called his boss. "What is a good law firm in the Phoenix area, Boss?"

"That would be Ross, Wagner and O'Malley," Richard Cooper replied without hesitation. "Why, do you need an attorney for something?"

"Not me, Boss. I met George Harris, Rick Stonewood's abandoned son, and he is a real nice kid. He is third year law school, near the top of his class with a need to make money quickly and move his mother from Kansas City to a warmer, drier climate. I hoped you might pull some strings, somehow," Red said hopefully.

"You, ah, don't think he has inherited any of his father's, ah, attributes?" Richard Cooper spoke rather hesitantly.

"Sure doesn't seem so, but I am sure any law firm would perform its own investigation," Red answered.

"I went to college with Winston Wagner," Cooper volunteered. "They are always looking for fresh, high quality young attorneys. He would even thank me for a good referral!"

George Harris saw Red when he entered the Student Lounge and stood up and waved to attract Red's attention. Red waved back and, after paying for a cup of coffee, joined him in a quiet corner of the Lounge. The two chitchatted for a bit, George told of a funny episode in class.

"What would you think of practicing law in Phoenix, George," Red inquired, when there was a lull in the conversation.

"Phoenix would be absolutely super," George enthused. "I could move Mom in with me, while I built up my income. Why do you ask? Do you know something?"

"Well, just an idea, I had. My boss knows one of the partners in a law firm there. He said that they are looking for new blood. It's all tentative, of course," Red replied.

"Wow! You met me yesterday and already, you are helping me find a job." George was smiling broadly.

"I am a bit impulsive," Red admitted. "We were talking on the phone; don't know how the subject came up, exactly.

"I have been praying for a position in a dry, warm climate. I have a couple of offers from New York City firms, with good starting salaries, but would hate to have to settle there," George declared. "Maybe this is the Lord's answer!"

It was Red's turn to be surprised. "Are you a Christian? Tell me about it." The dossier had not mentioned any religious affiliations!

"Not much to tell. I met this friend in high school. He was always talking about The Lord and how He loves

---

111

us." George paused for reflection. "I went to Church and Sunday school with him, and I told the Sunday school teacher, how I missed not having a father. She said that The Lord knew that I needed a father and that He would be my Heavenly Father, if I would ask. I knelt there and asked The Lord to be my father and to love me like He did my friend."

"Wow! Almost like it was all orchestrated by God," Red remarked tentatively.

"No question in my mind," George answered confidently. "I am going to start praying that this law firm in Phoenix will want me. What is the name of that firm, Red?"

"Ross, Wagner and O'Malley," Red replied.

George and Red met one more day before Red declared that he must go back to work. The two exchanged Email addresses and phone numbers, with George promising to let Red know, when he heard from the law firm, and Red promising to pray daily for a satisfactory outcome!

CHAPTER 19

The Threat Answered

Parker and the crew had fenced Echo Canyon, when Red returned, but all gates to the fenced watering places were left open. They would do no more trapping, until after the Muskrat Basin drive was over, and the herd culled.

J.B. Honeycutt had two dozen cowboys hired and wanted Red Iverson and his men there to meet them and organize them in preparation of culling the great herd. The merged crew met in a holding corral in town. They were all on horseback, as Red wanted to look at their mounts, who were being hired along with their masters.

"You men gather around me," Ben motioned the men to dismount.

"Your mounts all look serviceable, but I can't see how well they work. You all need to know that ninety-five percent of the job will be cutting out the culls and loading them in trucks. If that bronc, you're riding isn't a cutting horse, let me know now, cause you will be fired before noon, the first day. How about it?" Red paused for his words to sink in.

A slim Indian sidled forward. "My paint is a good horse, but he ain't no cuttin horse! I just needed the job!"

Red looked at the man in front of him. "What's your name, Dude?"

"Slim Walsh."

"Anyone got a spare mount to loan Slim?" Red cast an eye over the rest of the assembly!

An equally slim Indian stepped forward. "Slim, you can use Smokey, that mouse colored gelding of mine. He is a good cutter."

Both men looked at Red.

"And your name?"

"Charlie Simmons."

"Charlie, when you get paid, collect for two horses. And thanks, that is good of you."

An audible look of relief swept over Slim's face. "Thank you, Mister Iverson."

"You guys are to call me, Red. Okay! Question! I know you wranglers like to work on horseback, but I have several miles of corral fences to build. It is not hard work except for swinging a sledge to drive the iron stakes. Do you want the extra days work and build my corrals? Or do I hire some grunt labor?" Red looked around at the faces before him.

After a brief pause, Slim stepped forward. "I need the work, Red," he said quietly.

"Me, too," another voice spoke out.

A general muttering of approval took place until Red raised his hand.

"No stigma against you, but I need to know! Who doesn't want to build fence, raise your hand." One hand started up, but quickly was withdrawn!

After another pause, Red nodded. "Thanks men that saves my having to hire a second crew. Now, here is what we are going to do, and this is how we are going to do it!"

Red talked for more than a half hour, before he paused for questions. Thirty minutes later, he was finished.

"We gather out at the herd at daylight the morning after the drive. Are any of you participating in the drive?" Red looked around. No hand showed.

"Drovers Inc. doesn't hire local help," a bitter voice muttered.

Red nodded. "If anything develops that you can't show up. Please let me know as soon as possible. I am depending on each of you!"

As the men drifted away to their horses, Ben eased over to Red.

"That was well done, Boss." Ben's voice and demeanor was sober.

Red look over with surprise! "Why thank you, Ben, for that!"

Red and Parker drove out to the site of the great corral that was the apex of the great wild horse round-up. It was a well-planned choice in that it was a large amphitheater of two or three square miles. Most of the corral fence was up against some low foothills with five miles on each side of a giant funnel leading to the amphitheater. Fake evergreen foliage decorated the fences.

"I'm Stonewood. Who are--? Ah! You would be Red Iverson and his faithful sidekick, Parker. Glad to finally meet you face to face." Rick Stonewood spoke with just a hint of a sneer. "Waste of time, culling the herd! Ought to just load up the required quota and haul them off. None of these mustangs are worth a s--- anyhow!"

"Well, that is debatable, Mister Stonewood." Red's voice was still quiet and courteous. "Have you ever owned horses, Sir?"

"Just call me, Rick." His voice was irritable. "I never been on a horse in my life!"

Red's jaw dropped in surprise! "You mean, you don't know anything about horses?"

"What's to know? They got four legs and they stink! I don't have to like them to drive them." Stonewood dropped his civil tone. "I trust you have gotten my messages and are finding other employment, after you cull this herd for J.B. What your friends got was just a taste of what is available, should you continue your little horse trapping game!"

"Probably not, Mister Stonewood." Red retained his courteous demeanor. "You know, your son doesn't resemble you in the least!"

Rick, who was turning away, swung back with a grunt. "What do you know about my son?"

"Quite a bit, actually," Red answered. His tone

115

remained calm. "He is a very nice young man. Dedicated to his mother, a good Christian and in the top ten percent of his class. He should go far, if he isn't tainted by that SOB that sired him!"

Rick Stonewood's face was white and his hands, shaking. "You stay away from my son, or I will have you skinned alive!"

"On the contrary. I didn't put a snake in any of your friend's mailbox, slash any of your friend's tires or send a rape artist to attack a young innocent child. You did! Have you ever seen a dossier of yourself, Mister Stonewood?" Red's voice was now thick with repressed emotion. "You are probably too stupid to operate a computer. Have one of your minions look up your criminal history for you. I have made a dozen CDs of your dossier plus all the other rumors of your miserable life that are true, but unproven and," Red hand came from his pocket with a small tape recorder, "a copy of our recent conversation. Should any more threats occur against me or any of my friends, this will be sent to your son, the Arizona and Nevada State Police, and every major newspaper in the Nevada, Arizona area." Red's voice was hard and angry, now!

He wheeled and headed back to their truck.

"Good luck on your drive, Mister Stonewood," Parker said cheerfully, as he turned and followed Red.

CHAPTER 20

The Drive

Many of the quads and motorcycles had positioned themselves the day before in the far reaches of the area and in secluded canyons and camped there during the night. Daylight signaled the beginning of the drive as the unmuffled vehicles began their drive. The desert air soon rang from the sound of dozens of engines and dust clouds rose as the frightened horses fled from the noisy contraptions!

Two small helicopters circled the air above, occasionally swooping down to turn a wayward herd that had slipped by the wranglers. They were situated at opposite ends of the area. They also relayed information to those on the ground, regarding locations of isolated herds. Drovers Inc. was paid by the number of horses collected, so great pains were taken, not pass up any!

The giant arena, which was the destination of the drovers, was located in the south end of the Muskrat Basin, but to one side. The horses would be coming from a one hundred eighty degree fan, culminating at the entrance of the huge funnel, leading to the arena. The furthest horses would have over fifty miles to cover!

Red and his crew were not a part of the drive, but were parked near the large twelve hundred acre pen and were tuned in to the air to ground radio and able to follow some of the action. They could see huge dust clouds boiling upward in either direction, proof of many wild horses on the move.

The helicopter pilots had a unique task of directing, to a limited extent, the quads on the ground, plus doing their own part in the drive. Working at very low altitudes, a good part of their flight was at risk, and they were well paid for their work!

If they had had the time to appreciate it, a magnificent panorama was taking place below them! The horses presented a kaleidoscope of color as bright bays, sorrels, paints, dark blacks and every color in between, streamed at full speed across the prairie! Initially, the stallions attempted to keep their harems together, but as panic set in, it was each and every horse for themselves!

"Quad four. At your three o'clock, behind that small rise. Backtrack five hundred yards and circle right, around that rock hill to get behind them." The pilot's voice broke through the noise of his engine.

"Roger. Quad four!"

The quad, below the circling helicopter, did a quick U-turn and soon another group of wild horses joined the maelstrom of running horses. The panic spread ahead of the huge herd and new bands joined, taking the lead as the old leaders tired and began to lag.

Inexorably, the pounding hooves swept into the huge fenced funnel that would lead to capture and an end of the wild life for many of the horses. Miles further back, the tired horses had to be driven. Their eyes still rolled in fear, but exhaustion slowly replaced panic, as the acres and acres of horses slowed to a trot ahead of the tenacious quads.

Red and his crew were stationed well back from the apex of the funnel. They watched the leaders thunder into the two square mile pen.

"Well, this is certainly faster than our system," Parker muttered as the horses poured by them.

"Some nice stock in there," Ben added.

"I saw a pinto mare, I'd like to have." Trace looked over at Red, hopefully.

"You need a mate for that stud," Micah agreed. "You better start saving your pennies!"

By three o'clock, the flood had thinned and the tired laggards began to arrive.

"Red, that sorrel has a broken front leg," Ben cried out.

"I see her," Red replied grimly. "There are going to be a bunch of injured broncos, before this drive is over!"

The pace was slower and slower as the end of the vast herd appeared, several miles away. Many limping horses were noticeable as the herd thinned. The sound of the quads was easily discernible and they could be seen, darting here and there, through the dust clouds. The two helicopters rose above the melee below them and turned toward town! Their work was done!

The sun had set, as the last of the vast herd straggled through the narrow opening to the corral and a dozen rushed to carry the panels to close the gap. The round-up was over!

"Now the real work begins," Red muttered to himself, as he surveyed the large mass of horseflesh.

He turned to his crew.

"It's supper and bed. We have a long day tomorrow!"

"And the next day and the next day," added Parker, as he climbed into the driver's seat.

CHAPTER 21

Cleaning Up

"Charlie Simmons, pick out ten men and start carrying panels for the corrals as we laid them out. Trace, grab three sledgehammers, and men, and start driving the posts. Micah, you're in charge of setting the panels. You need at least six men. Ben, go with Charlie and, when he gets one of the big pens finished, take four of the men and start running horses in. Twenty to thirty head. I should have a small loading pen done by that time and we can start filling it with culls." Red beckoned for the remaining men to come with him and then stopped.

"Parker, work with these guys and show them how to lock the panels together. Once we have a loading chute set up, help the drivers back into place. Let's go!"

It was mid-morning, when Ben crowded two dozen horses into the completed large holding pen. Ben, with the help of one of the wranglers, held four choice mares in one corner, while Red and the others crowded the remainder into a waiting rig for transport to city. The second holding was completed by then and Ben filled it with another group of wild horses.

At three o'clock, one semi-trailer pulled away with the first load of culls. All the pens had been set up, with a fine stallion in one of the smaller pens, waiting for four more choice mares to complete his harem. Red's crew was in full production.

The second semi-trailer pulled away from the loading chute, as the sun touched the horizon, and Red called his men in.

"You guys did great today. I didn't expect to get this much done the first day. Get a good night's rest. and I'll see you tomorrow."

The success of the first day did not carry over to the second day! It started with a "no show" from one of the semi-trailer rigs! Red waited until the first rig pulled away with his load of culls, before calling J.B. Both loading pens and one holding pen was filled with culls, awaiting transportation. The second holding pen was occupied by a black stallion and eleven mares.

The other semi-trailer rig finally arrived, but the driver was still under the effect of alcohol and Red wouldn't load him, and sent him away,

The original semi-trailer and the replacement arrived at the same time, after an hour of waiting, and one was quickly loaded and sent into town. Things went smoothly as the second load was gathered and separated and loaded.

Then misfortune struck again. An angry, frustrated stallion turned on an unsuspecting gelding! The gelding was bruised, but unhurt. The rider was trapped briefly with his leg under his fallen mount, and it was badly bruised. Red sent the rider to the hospital with Micah in his truck, and the process continued.

"Red, Ben isn't coming in with the last drive," Parker called to Red over the noise.

"Are you sure?"

"Yeah! He was riding that iron grey of his this morning. He's not with those riders." Parker was insistent!

Before Red could respond, a faint pop was heard in the distance. A few minutes later, a second pop sounded.

Red waved for his crew to continue and walked over to join Parker.

"Those were pistol shots," Parker mentioned, unnecessarily!

Red nodded and after a few more minutes, pointed

toward the big pasture. Ben, on his iron grey gelding was galloping up. He continued on over to where Red and Parker were standing and slid off his horse.

"I just killed a couple of horses," he muttered. His voice was low and angry. "The one with a broken leg was lying down and couldn't get up. All swollen up with the bone sticking out," he continued. "Saw a mare for the first time. Apparently ran into a broken branch and opened up her stomach." Ben looked like he may be sick.

"I'll call for a backhoe and get them buried. Thanks, Ben. I know that wasn't easy." Red turned and went back to loading culls.

The final blow of the day occurred as the last semi-trailer pulled away from the loading chute! The right front tire blew , and the combined strength of two men could not break loose the lug nuts to change the tire! The tired wranglers had to break down the loading chute and extend the corral out to the rig. There, the gate to the trailer was opened and the horses were forced to jump to the ground and were put back in the loading pen for the night.

The repair truck was pulling away as Red arrived the next morning, and the loading chute was quickly set up and the semi-trailer reloaded. Simultaneously with the semi's departure, Ben, with his crew increased to a dozen, drove in a pen full of mustangs.

Red's phone rang as the culling began. He motioned for Parker to take over and moved away from the noise to answer it. It was J.B.

"How are things going, Red?"

"Had some glitches yesterday. Hope things will go a little smoother, today. Should clean them up tomorrow. I'm guessing that we will have more culls, than we are scheduled to keep. Do I keep culling or release the rest of the horses when I reach the eleven hundred mark?"

"How many more culls do you think you will have, Red," J.B. inquired.

"I am guessing at least two hundred," Red replied.

"When you reach thirteen hundred culls, release the rest," J.B. directed. "Had another reason to call. A truck from the Wyoming State Honor Farm will arrive around noon. They need around twenty horses. Give them the top end of the culls, if possible."

"I'll take care of them, J.B."

The wranglers had just finished their catered noon meal when the Honor Farm semi-trailer arrived. Red waved them over to the loading chute where he had their load picked out for them. When a slim young man climbed out of the passenger side, Slim Walsh jumped to his feet.

"That's my brother," he exclaimed and trotted over to greet him.

After a hug and a brief conversation, Slim returned to the group and his brother walked on to the loading chute. Two of Red's loading crew had already joined Red and were mounting up to load the horses.

"What is the State Honor Farm," one of the wranglers asked Slim.

"It is a rehab program for minimum security prisoners. They work with wild horses to gentle them and eventually sell them," Slim answered him. "My brother went through the program and returned as instructor. He has always been good with horses."

"Well this isn't getting any horses in the pen," Parker prodded them and headed for the saddled horses.

Working the horses herd resumed. The wilder ones had evaded being driven up to this point. Ben needed more riders to push them into the cutting pens. Toward the middle of the afternoon, he dismounted to talk to Red.

"Red, we got some hurt mustangs out here. I hated to leave them suffer, but couldn't get them sorted out of the wild bunch without running them and hurting them further. I have been pushing them to one side to date, but now the herd is thinned out, I'd like to try to bring them in and get a veterinarian working on them. I would like most all the riders to help so as to keep them from trying to run around me."

"Sure, Ben. Take all my crew and half of Parker's. I'll get on the phone and try to get a vet out ASAP!" Red slid his phone out as Ben collected his wranglers.

Soon a crowd of twenty riders trotted out of the loading area. The wild horses fled from in front of them, but they held a slow, steady trot to the far side of the pasture. Their goal was easily discernible from the other horses, as several were lying down, and others standing with drooping heads!

"Damn them and their big drives!" Angry mutters were heard as the riders formed a half circle around the thirty some horses and urged them toward the cutting pens. A few half-hearted plunges were made by some of the injured mustangs, but the large number of drivers discouraged most of the escape attempts!

Slowly and quietly, the wranglers urged the limping herd into a holding pen to await the veterinarian. The sobered riders went back to their respective tasks, and the culling continued.

It was almost quitting time, when a pick-up arrived, and two men got out and approached the loading pens. Red dismounted and met them.

"We're vets," one of them announced, shortly! "Understand you have some injured mustangs!"

Wordless, Red led them to the pen, containing the injured horses.

"Damn! What was this, a mass torture project," the vet burst out.

"Just for the record," Red said evenly, "neither me nor my men had anything to do with the drive that caused these injuries."

"Well, why did you wait so long to have them treated? They have been hurting!" The venom in his voice lessened noticeably, but was still there!

"There were over twenty seven hundred mustangs in that pasture! They were thick as fleas on a dog's back! I would have had to run the hurt ones to get them out of the herd. You think that would have been a good thing?" Red's voice showed that he was running out of patience! "By gathering them together quietly, one at a time, we were able to get them in the pen without any fuss!"

The vet answered after a short pause. "I apologize. I jumped to conclusions. I'll shut up and get to work."

"I see you have a squeeze chute on your truck," Red replied in a normal tone of voice. "I can have my men erect some panels to it."

"Thanks. We'll back it in. We have a hydraulic lift to get it off and it is mechanized." The two vets headed back to their truck.

"Micah, you and Trace grab a couple of guys and set up some panels for the docs," Red called as he went back to his crew. "Knock off for the day, when you are finished."

Red's crew had been at work for two hours before the veterinarians were on the job. Working with only two pens slowed the operation, plus the wildest were the last to be driven in, but shortly after noon lunch, Parker called to Red!

"That is one thousand, three hundred and seven culls, Red, counting the mares in the sick pen. My tally is one thousand thirty-one released back on the range, including forty-one stallions."

"We will finish loading this semi and the one that is waiting," Red replied. "I hope to release most of the injured back in the range, if the vet concurs. Hate the thought of trying to get them in the truck without hurting them further!"

CHAPTER 22

Red Repents

J.B. Honeycutt sat across a small scarred desk from Red and Parker.

"You and your crew did a fine job, Red," he was saying. "I expected it to take longer."

Red had finished loading the last semi-trailer by three o'clock, and had released the remaining wild horses back to the desert range, and sent the riders home with instructions to check in with him in the morning.

"Thanks, J.B. There are some loose ends, and I wanted to know, how you wanted me to handle it. There is that pen full of injured horses. Some probably need more medical attention, while others could be released. I am reluctant to crowd them in a truck, just yet. They need water!"

"The veterinarian is supposed to contact me today. I will follow his recommendations." J.B. made a note for himself. "Could you recommend any of the men, I hired to stay with me and eventually run a program, such as you have for Cooper?"

"Charlie Simmons." Red did not hesitate. "He accepts responsibility easily and gets along with his crew. I was going to suggest that you turn over the knocking down of the pens and the two long drift fences to him. Walt Wiley, who is still recovering from an accident with the horses, and his brother, Ben, who shows real good promise, would both be candidates."

"Good." J.B. made another note to himself. "Would you have this Charlie Simmons drop in to see me, first thing tomorrow? Anything else?"

"Those two dead horses. The backhoe never did show up!" Red reminded him. "There is a report form for me to fill out, too, I believe."

"To be sure! There is always a form." J.B. pushed the intercom button. "Rachel, could you locate the form for mercy killing of a protected animal?"

"What a relief with that behind us," Red remarked as they left the office. "It will be good to get back to camp. I'll call in to the boss, and we can head out. Reckon Ben is already gone!"

When Red and Parker arrived at the base camp, one of the quads was gone and a note from Ben indicated that he was going to check out the fenced watering spots for wild horses. Ben drove in as Parker was preparing supper.

"Lot of horse tracks at Wolf Creek and Echo Canyon. Looks like only one herd is frequenting The Seeps and three herds are watering at Willow Creek." Ben reported. "Raidy's Springs is so heavily trampled, it is hard to tell. There are some fresh horse tracks, though."

"Thanks for checking them out for me, Ben. Tomorrow is Sunday. We will stake out Wolf Creek on Monday night," Red responded. "How is Beth doing, after her ordeal?"

Ben grinned wryly. "You know, she is more angry than traumatized! She seems to think, if she had gotten a couple more licks with her car keys, he would have slunk away!"

"Well, I am glad she feels that way," Red grinned in return. "Not sure that I agree with her thinking though! He sounded like a tough character."

Parker's call to supper interrupted their conversation.

"You going in to see Irene, tonight, Red?" Parker was talking between mouthfuls.

"Yes. Walt was going to try to meet me there. Irene is still staying with Teresa."

"I'm supposed to relieve Walt. He is still staying with Beth and those two security guys are there, too. Why don't you spend the evening with us, Parker," Ben broke in. "You can get Beth to laugh some. Help her forget."

"Do that, Parker," Red urged. "I got some time. I'll clean up here. You guys go on."

Walt's pick-up was already parked in front of Teresa's house, when Red arrived.

Irene greeted Red with a warm kiss. "I am so glad you are safe! I worry about you and that Stonewood monster."

"Red, would you mind just staying in this evening and playing cards," Teresa asked, after the greetings were over.

"I gave the security guys off until one o'clock," Walt added. "Pinochle okay with everyone?"

"Sounds great to me," Red readily agreed. "An evening of relaxation is just what the doctor ordered!"

"Now don't relax too much, if you are going to be my partner," Irene warned, to the other's amusement.

Walt was dealing the first hand, when Red decided to break the good news.

"I don't think we have to worry about Rick Stonewood doing any of us bodily harm," he remarked nonchalantly.

Walt stopped with his hand in midair. "What do you mean? What happened?"

"Well, I did a little detective work on Mister Stonewood and found a few facts about him, plus a lot of rumors!" Red was enjoying the suspense that he was causing and continued to relate all that he had found, his trip to Princeton University and the subsequent conversation with Stonewood.

"He just tiptoed away. From the look on his face, I think, our troubles with him are over," Red finished, smugly!

The reaction to Red's recital was somewhat different than Red had expected as he looked around the table. Walt's face wore a look of immense satisfaction. Teresa showed a complete lack of emotion. Her gaze was fixed on Irene.

Red's smugness dissolved as he observed Irene's expression. It was a mixture of surprise, hurt and disapproval!

"Oh Darling! You couldn't! You wouldn't," Irene burst out.

"What do you mean," responded a bewildered Red.

"The son! It would ruin his life to find out about his father that way!" Irene was almost in tears.

"I didn't mean that I would actually tell him," Red muttered.

"But your witness! You are a professed Christian! What must he think," Irene pursued.

The room was quiet for several uncomfortable minutes.

"Walt, weren't you dealing the cards," Teresa broke the silence.

"Ah, yes. Lost track of where I was." Walt gathered up the cards and commenced to deal again.

"You are under for fifteen," Teresa informed Irene, "and I'll bid sixteen."

Conversation was somewhat forced for a few hands. Finally, Walt laid down his hand.

"She is right, you know, Red. Even after what Beth went through, I gotta say, we can't be like them. At first, I agreed with you and I sure didn't feel like turning the other cheek! But Irene nailed it."

Red turned to Irene. "It seemed right at the time, and, I confess, it didn't occur to me how it would go down with George Harris. I will get in to see Rick Stonewood as soon as I can,, and withdraw my threat, and give him the stash of CDs. I hope that I can convince him that he is off the hook!"

"Oh, thank you, Red." Irene's face became stricken. "I hope---."

"Not at all, Darling. It took courage to confront me! I am glad that you did?"

"I have this urge for something ice creamy," Teresa interjected. "How's about we slip down to the Dairy Queen for a treat?"

"Done," Walt cried! "Teresa is driving and I am buying!"

Laughing the four headed for the door.

Monday night at Wolf Creek proved successful and a large herd was captured. Several fine mares were in the harem and some equally fine yearlings and two year olds. The stallion was a dark blood bay of good quality, but older.

It was decided to send the culls to town, as usual, but transport the keepers to the Seeps, as there was not much activity there.

"Red, have you been watching the weather forecasts," Parker inquired as they drove back to camp.

"No I haven't, Parker. And I should be," Red replied. "What's coming?"

"Bad early winter storm! Lots of moisture, up to six inches of snow tomorrow night and temperatures dropping into the low twenties!" Parker sounded like a radio weatherman.

"Might be the end of trapping the herds at the water holes," Red mused. "We may have to start throwing hay to them, if the snow stays around. I'll ask the boss to send out a couple semis of baled hay!"

"Looks like a cold job, working the horses. Hope we get the pens up tomorrow, before the storm hits! I don't know about you guys, but I am moving my sleeping bag into the tent tonight," Ben declared!

The temperature was hovering around freezing, as they worked to separate the culls and snowflakes began to appear, as they loaded them.

"Parker, toss a couple of bales on the quad and bring them back." Red called as he climbed into the cab. "We won't try to move the others to the Seeps, until the storm is past!"

The snowfall thickened as Red began his drive to town. Soon it was difficult to ascertain, where the road was. Red drove slowly, stopping occasionally to insure that he was, indeed, on the road. He breathed a sigh of relief, when the main road came in sight! Even though it was only early afternoon, all of the occasional cars were driving slowly with headlights on.

The yard personnel had waited for him, even though it was full dark, when he arrived. As they unloaded his trailer, Red called both the camp and his boss to assure them that he had arrived safely, and that he would stay the night there and return home the next day.

Red did not return the following day! The first day's snow was wet and stuck where it fell, but as the temperature fell, the second day and the snow became dry and the rising wind carried the snow across the desert with the visibility close to zero!

Bright sunlight greeted Red as he emerged from his motel room the third day! The temperature was in the teens, but promised to warm up rapidly. He quickly bolted down his breakfast and started back to camp.

"Haw!" Was Parker's greeting as Red stepped down from the truck cab. "Fine thing! You loll around town, sleep in a nice warm motel room, while your troops freeze their tails in a tent!"

"The military has this saying 'rank has its privileges'," Red responded. "Besides, your tail would not have been any warmer if mine was freezing, too."

"Well, maybe not," Parker conceded, "but I would have enjoyed freezing my tail, more!"

"Another bad breath in the tent with me, would not have made my night any pleasanter," Ben averred. "You are off the hook with me, Boss."

"Well, I am glad somebody appreciates my efforts to enliven your lives," was Red's final contribution!

"We just got back from Wolf Creek," Parker stated. "No problem there! Those mustangs went through the storm in fine shape. It was love at first bite with those hay bales!"

"Good! We will take a bale with us to coax them up the ramp. We will move them to the Seeps today. While Parker and I do that, Ben, would you check and see, if there is any activity at the other pens, and if the mustangs are getting any forage, through the snow," Red directed.

The small propane heater struggled to maintain a livable temperature in the tent that night. Red and Parker had successfully moved the mares and stallion to the Seeps. The taller grass around the Springs would sustain the small herd for several weeks, if necessary. Ben had reported minimum activity around the other fenced watering spots.

The men were in a deep discussion regarding the future, when Red's phone rang.

"Red, this is George Harris."

"George, how are you? How is school coming?"

"Well, I am not in school at this minute, I am in a motel room in Phoenix, Arizona." George's voice sounded excited. "I had an interview with Ross, Wagner and O'Malley this afternoon and they agreed to take me on as a junior partner, if things work out!"

"Wow! That is great news! When do you start?"

"That is the great part, Red. I am going to take the test for a para-legal, certified in Arizona, and work for them next summer. I still have another year, here at Princeton, and, of course, I need to pass the bar examination, before I am a full-fledged attorney. They have even offered to help me prepare for that! I can't began to thank you for putting me in touch with Mister Wagner! He is a true man of God. Wish I could have had a father like him!"

"I am so happy for you, George!" Red was grinning from ear to ear to his companions. "How about your mother? Will you move her to Phoenix?"

"That's another thing, Red. Mom is only forty-two. Mister Wagner suggested that he could give me an advance on my salary, and give Mom a chance to get her high school diploma and perhaps train for a more meaningful career. If she wants to, that is. Maybe a legal secretary or something!"

"Sounds like your trail ahead is pretty straight, George," Red responded. "When you get settled in next summer, give me a call. You will be a lot closer, then. I could maybe drop in for a visit."

"That was Stonewood's son," Parker inquired, after Red put away his phone.

"It was." Red moved a little closer to the heater. "The boss put a law firm that he knows in Phoenix in touch with him. Apparently, they hit it off, and they hired him." Red went on to give them the particulars.

"Must be great to have brains," was Ben's input.

"Now, Ben. You want to be a lawyer? I get an email about once a week to the effect that for four hundred ninety five dollars, you can sign up to study for the bar exam," Parker expanded. "They guarantee that you pass, or you can keep taking their courses, until you do. You don't need to spend fifty thousand to attend Princeton University!"

"Ha, ha," laughed Ben. "I would still taking their courses at ninety years old!"

"Just trying to help," Parker pretended to have hurt feelings.

CHAPTER 23

Hay for the Horses

Having slept fully dressed, the men were not too discomforted, when the heater ran out of fuel. Red was the first to stir and had the coffee ready, when Ben and Parker emerged from the tent.

"Gonna be warmer, today," was Red's encouraging words of greeting.

Ben, as usual headed immediately for the horses, who were patiently waiting their bale of hay. The sun was just peeking over the horizon.

Parker grunted as he poured his coffee. "My time to make breakfast, Red. You drink your coffee and figure out, what we are going to do today!"

"Think I have got a handle on it, Parker," Red replied. "I will wait until Ben gets back."

"I was thinking over trapping the herds with hay," Red began, when all were on their last cup of coffee. "Those mustangs don't know a bale of hay from a rocking chair, at this point! If we show up with some bales of hay with the trailer or the quads, they will split to the next county."

"What if we just amble up wind of them, a quarter mile or so, and open a bale to see if they can get a whiff of the dried hay. We leave and hope they wander over to see what smells so good. Horses are pretty smart, and if they are hungry, after a couple of bales, they may let us get close enough to feed them. They are hooked! We can lead them to a corral now!"

"Worth a try, Red," was Parker's response.

"I think it will work, Boss." Ben was more positive!

The air was crisp, but the sun was warming up, when the two quads departed with four square bales of hay stacked on the back. Ben was leading toward the area, where he had seen the most activity. It was an hour, before they spotted their first herd. Still a mile away, they could see the mustangs pawing the snow to uncover some sparse grass.

Ben led to the up wind quadrant and began a slow approach toward the herd. The sound of the quiet engines was quickly audible to the herd and they stopped their labor to watch the approaching vehicles. The grey stallion trotted a few paces toward them.

As the stud nervously showed sign of moving away, Ben stopped. Parker hopped off and, cutting the twine holding the bale together, he began to walk away from the quad, shaking chunks from the bale. Ben did the same from the other quad.

Having spread the bales, they sat in the quads and waited, while the light breeze carried the scent of dry hay to the stallion. Minutes past, some of the mares returned to pawing in the snow. Suddenly the stallion was seen to stretch out his nose! The scent of hay had arrived! He moved a few steps closer.

"Let's go," Red ordered and the pair moved slowly away from the two bales of hay. They proceeded about a half mile before halting again to watch. The stallion was walking slowly toward the hay. Step one completed for that herd.

Using the same technique, they fed two more herds.

"Boss, we are pretty close to Echo Canyon," Ben proposed. "Why don't we leave the last bales at the entrance?"

At Red's nod, Ben turned toward the Canyon. The sun was beginning to melt the snow in sheltered places. With the hay unloaded, the wranglers returned to base camp.

———

After a late lunch, Red called Richard Cooper.

"Boss, I would like to run over to Las Vegas and talk to Rick Stonewood. We had some disagreements, and I would like to smooth them over. I would be gone a couple days and would get Trace to sub for me, when I am gone. If that is all right with you."

"You take what time you need, if you can ease the tension with Stonewood, Red. How is this weather effecting your operation?"

"The horses are pretty much ignoring the watering spots, for now, Boss," Red replied. "We started spreading some bales of hay. I think we can use hay to trap them, with a little training."

"You want to keep a close eye on the weather, Red," Mister Cooper warned! "Wyoming can cook up some bad storms, moving fast. Anything I can do to assist, call me!"

"Boss says to watch out for fast moving winter storms," Red mentioned, after he had rang off. "Good advice! Reminds me! You two get busy packing bales around our sleeping tent. Three high should stop the wind from blowing under the flap and form a small windbreak for us. Parker, check our stash of propane tanks. Ben call Trace and see if he would like to help us out for a few days, while I am at Las Vegas."

"Typical commanding officer," Parker griped. "Leave us freeze our buns in the desert, while he hits the casinos in the big city!"

"Aw, you are just getting too soft, Parker," Red grinned. "A little frost on your sleeping bag will do you good. Besides, it's not my fault Drovers Inc. has its offices in Las Vegas!"

"Red Iverson to see Mister Stonewood." Red told the receptionist. He had driven into Las Vegas the preceding day and called for an appointment.

"Please be seated," the attractive redhead instructed him. "I will let Mister Stonewood know you are here!"

That he was kept waiting a good twenty minutes, did not surprise Red. That he was able to make an appointment at all, was due to Stonewood's obvious curiosity! Finally, the receptionist announced that, "Mister Stonewood can see you, now."

"What brings you here, Iverson? You looking for a job?" Rick Stonewood's voice carried a sneer. He sat behind an unpretentious desk in a sparsely furnished office. He obviously spent very little time there.

"No, Mister Stonewood, I came to bring you these." Red laid a stack of DVDs on the desk before him. "These are all the copies of your dossier, with my comments and our taped conversation that day. I am withdrawing my threats and apologizing for making them!" Red sat down in a chair, in front of the desk, without invitation!

Rick picked up one of the discs and fingered it a few moments, then pressed the intercom button to the receptionist.

"Miss Hodges, would you bring me a DVD player?"

The two men sat in silence, until the receptionist entered with a DVD player. She plugged it in and inserted the disc that her employer was holding and turned it on. She then left the office.

"Ricky Stonewood was adopted by an English couple--." Red's voice came through the speaker, clearly and Rick Stonewood reached over and shut it off.

"Okay! Assuming you don't have another dozen stashed away somewhere, what's it go going to cost me?"

"There is no cost involved, Mister Stonewood. I simply regretted my actions and am attempting to undo them," Red averred.

"Do you expect me to believe that?"

"Yes, as a matter of fact, I do. I am a professed Christian, a follower of Jesus Christ and I try to handle situations the way He would want me to. I don't think I did that, in this case." Red looked and sounded sincere.

"I can't believe it! You believe all that garbage?" Rick sat back in his chair, as if struck.

"Yes, I believe that garbage, as you call it. And I also believe in Heaven and Hell." Red started to rise, but then sat back. "I have some good news about your son, George. I want to tell you!"

Rick's face clouded up! "I told you to stay away from

my son!" He started to stand.

Red held up his hand. "Wait. This is news, you will be glad to hear!"

Rick regained his seat, his looks a mixture of anger and curiosity.

"George called me from Phoenix a couple nights ago. He has been accepted into the law firm of Ross, Wagner and O'Malley. He expects to work for them next summer and then full time, when he finishes school. He will become a junior partner, when he passes the Bar Examination!"

The anger slowly faded from Rick's face, to be replaced by pride!

"My son, an attorney!"

Red stood up. "Just thought you would like to know."

Rick waved him back. "Wait a minute. That is one of the most prestigious firms in Arizona! How did they come to hire George?"

"My boss, Mister Cooper went to school with Mister Wagner," Red admitted. "But he only introduced them. George got the position on his own merits!"

Rick rubbed his chin thoughtfully. "Maybe I have been a little hasty about you. You don't have to worry about any harm to your friends!"

"Thank you. I do appreciate that," Red responded, and then hesitated. "Would you like to see a picture of your son?"

"You have a picture of George?" Rick's eyes lit up.

Red worked with his cell phone a bit and then handed it to Rick. "We are in the Student Lounge. The others were just outside."

Rick studied the photos intently. "He is a good looking young man!" At Red's nod of confirmation. "He looks like his mother." His tone carried a touch of regret!

Red said nothing as Rick returned the cell phone. He stood up to leave and walked toward the door.

"There is one thing, Mister Stonewood. That garbage about Christianity, which you mentioned. Your son believes it, too." Red closed the door behind him.

CHAPTER 24

Thanksgiving

The camp was empty when Red arrived mid-afternoon. The truck and trailer were there, but both quads were gone.

Red unloaded his gear and noticed how neatly the bales of hay had been stacked around the sleeping tent. He stopped just inside the tent and gaped with astonishment! The tent floor had been neatly divided into small cubicles with hay bales. Hanging above one cubicle was a sign that read "The Boss"! A thick mat of hay covered the floor under where his sleeping bag lay!

Chuckling, Red dropped his gear on his sleeping bag and returned to the kitchen tent, where he commenced to prepare supper. Dusk was approaching, when he heard the sound of the two quads arriving.

"Whoopee! The boss is back," yelled Parker as he wheeled his quad into camp. "You will never guess what happened, Red!" He rushed to get under the big umbrella heater.

"I give up," Red laughed. "What happened?"

"That Ben is a wonder, Red! The spot, where we dumped the first bales of hay, was clean as a bird's beak the next morning and a couple of herds were sorta hanging around and they got interested as soon as we broke out some hay." Parker was warming up to his tale. "Ben suggested we break up some bales around the quads, and just sit there, instead of driving off. Well, we sat there for thirty or forty minutes and the horses keep edging closer, until one of the old mares got a bit of hay, and then the whole herd dove into that hay and paid us no attention."

"When the whole herd had their heads down and their mouths full, Ben lit off his quad and just eased it out of the herd. We did the same on the other spot with much the same result."

"Let me tell the rest," Ben cut in. "We went out this morning and sure enough, those mustangs were waiting for us and even came to meet us! This time, instead of stopping and feeding them, Trace got on the bales and just dropped a small bunch at a time, while I headed for Echo Canyon. Parker saw what was happening and pulled away to the other spot, where a herd was waiting for him!"

"The same thing happened there, Red," Parker broke in. "And I started leading that bunch of mustangs toward Echo Canyon. When I got there, I was leading about twenty head, and there was Ben out in the middle of the corral feeding a whole slew of horses!"

"Boss, we got over sixty head of horses locked up in Echo Canyon," Ben said impressively!

"Whaat!" Red dropped the cup of coffee that he had just poured!

"It's a fact, Red! I counted sixty-seven head," Parker corroborated.

"Wow! I should go back to Las Vegas, while you guys trap horses for me. I don't know what to say!" Red poured another cup of coffee and sat down. "I should have prepared a real feast, but there is just spaghetti and meatballs."

"That sounds like a feast to me, Boss," Trace interrupted. "If you don't mind, I will just help myself, while these guys pat themselves on the back! I'm starved!"

"You're right, Trace. It is supper time, and the toast is going to be more than just toast," Red jumped to his feet. "You guys wash up, while I dish up!"

"Hey, Boss, how do you like your new digs," Trace, inquired between bites.

"Why, what do you mean, Trace? My new digs!" Red's expression was baby innocent!

"Aw! You haven't been in the sleeper tent?" Trace was deflated!

"Well, yes, I threw my gear in there," Red replied. "Come to think of it, I noticed some hay in there. Is that to keep them dry?"

Parker's face began to work and Ben broke into a chuckle, when Trace finally caught on that his leg was being pulled.

"Aw, Boss!"

"Seriously, Trace. If that was you, it was a great job. Give us some privacy, and it will be a lot warmer in there," Red came to his rescue. "Thanks a lot! Especially for the hay under my sleeping bag."

"You are welcome, Boss." Trace was mollified and had another helping of spaghetti to show, there was no hard feeling.

"And if there is a pinto mare that you like in that herd, it's yours." Red tossed in.

"You mean it, Boss?" Trace's grin was a mile wide. At Red's nod, "just for that, I'll do up the dishes for you!"

"You haven't told us about your visit with Rick Stonewood, Boss," Ben suggested.

"Actually, I feel pretty good about it," Red responded and continued to relate the conversation with Stonewood to them! "I feel pretty confident that we can remove the guards from the girls and that they are no longer in danger from Rick Stonewood."

"Odd how human nature is," Parker mentioned. "How such a jerk to everyone else can still have a soft spot for a son, whom he has hardly, if ever, seen!"

Red drove the truck and trailer over to Echo Canyon the next morning. Besides the material for the loading pens, they carried enough hay for two days' feed. The driving of stakes went slow into the frozen ground, even with Trace operating the sledgehammer. They did finish before dark, and left a broken bale in the loading pen, with the gate open, in hopes they could catch a quick truckload, the next morning.

"It's going to take three or four loads, this time, Red," Parker opined.

"Yes," Red agreed, "and I want to save one of those studs in Raidy's Springs. We will turn that roan stallion back out with, whatever good mares we have."

"Boss, has it occurred to you that that roan stud will hang out here all winter now, waiting to be fed," Ben inquired.

"Yeah, Ben, it has. I'm thinking we can lead him away, just like you led him here and establish permanent feeding grounds several miles from here or we will lose all usage of Echo Canyon!"

The next morning, the loading pen was full of milling mustangs, each trying to get a bite of hay! It was just a matter of cutting out a few of the choice mares and tossing a bale of hay in the trailer. The culls crowded up the ramp and the loading was complete!

"Wow! That was the easiest load, yet," Parker proclaimed.

"I'll say," Red agreed. "I have a head start, maybe I can get back early. Parker, you and Trace can cut that brown stallion into the loading pen and I could haul him to Raidy's Springs yet today. Ben, leave your horse with them, and I will drop you off at camp. I want you to take a quad and my telescope up to Lookout Point and pinpoint all the herds, you can on one of the maps. If we are to start a feeding program, I need to know where to set up at!"

On the return trip of Red's second load of culls, he carried a third quad and a small wagon, made for hauling bales. Richard Cooper had insisted on sending them! He also reminded Red that next week was Thanksgiving Day and instructed him to feed the horses the day before and to stay in camp that day. He did not elaborate or invite questions!

With all the culls transported into town, the wranglers concentrated on winning over several herds to the sight of the quads carrying hay bales. With the map, provided by Ben, they established feeding sites, as close to the fenced water holes as possible.

Thanksgiving Day arrived clear and cold! The wranglers slept late and rose to hang round camp, expectantly!

It was close to noon, when Ben suddenly stopped and held up a hand! "That's Walt's pickup! Another vehicle with him!"

"That's so," Trace seconded him. "I think the other is a jeep!"

Walt's pickup rolled on into camp and stopped at the table near the kitchen. Beth erupted from the passenger side and ran over to Ben, to give him a big hug. Irene stepped from Teresa's jeep and gave Red an equally big one.

"Happy Thanksgiving," Teresa announced and unloaded several pies on the table.

Walt wasted no time lifting a large, insulated, food carrier from his vehicle. "How about a little help, here," he directed to the gaping wranglers.

In short order, a tablecloth was whisk over the scarred picnic table and a steaming roast turkey with all the usual trimming were crowded on it. A stack of plates with utensils held down one end.

Teresa, who was apparently orchestrating the celebration, took a last look around. "Did we forget anything?"

"Just the Lord's blessing," Walt replied and held out a hand to her.

The others took the hint an all joined hands.

"Lord, what a pleasure it is to give You thanks, today. Not only for this scrumptious feast, and we do thank you for that, but for a blessing filled season! I want to especially thank You for Your touch on my body, that I have complete recovery with no lasting effects from my accident with the horses. Then, I want to express my appreciation for Your sending Teresa to me and for her returning my love. And now that You brought us together, Lord, I ask for Your continued touch on our lives, and that we will always hear Your voice."

———

"Again, Lord, we thank you for this food, your blessing on the ones that prepared it, and those that are about to consume it! Amen!"

Walt looked up to find the circle of questioning eyes upon him. Teresa wore a noticeable blush.

"If you will forgive me for holding up our repast a few more minutes, I would like to present this to my fiancée!" Walt pulled a small black box from his pocket and opening it, he slipped a diamond ring on Teresa's finger!

Teresa's surprised, "Oh" was followed by the oohs and aahs of the two girls, who rushed to her side to admire the ring.

"Could we eat now," Trace complained! "I'm starved."

The men moved out of the sleeping tent, leaving it for the three women. Ben and Walt combined their talents to make breakfast on Friday morning, while Parker and Trace loaded the quads with hay bales. Walt and Teresa took the quad with the trailer, and Trace went with them to show the way and do the heavy work. Red and Irene drove the second one and Parker, Ben and Beth occupied the last one. They set out to feed the wild horses.

Red and Irene fed two herds near Wolf Creek, staying parked in the midst of the scattered hay. The horses were reluctant to approach, but hunger finally won out and they began to move freely around the quad. The horses spooked momentarily, when Red restarted the quad, but went immediately back to feeding!

"Are you ready for a good climb, Irene," Red asked as they drove way. "I would like to climb Lookout Point before we go back."

Irene shivered slightly. "I am getting a little cold. Some exercise would help."

Halfway up the slope to Lookout Point, Irene panted to a stop. "Okay! I'm warmed up now, could we go back?"

Red laughed. "We will take five minutes rest here, and then you can hang onto my bag, and I'll pull you!"

"Oh, Red! This is lovely!" Irene struggled up the last

steps and gazed around.

The air was clear and visibility was unlimited. Some snow still lay in sheltered spots. Dark spots, which were wild horses, were visible in every direction.

"Wait until I get the telescope set up," Red responded, as he clipped the legs in place.

"Oh my! There are still a lot of horses out there! How many have you taken away," Irene asked.

"Around three hundred fifty, I think," Red replied. "Mister Cooper wants me to take away at least fifteen hundred. The experts tell us the range will only support around a thousand head."

Irene gave the telescope back to Red.

"Hey! There is that blue roan stallion! The first one we trapped. I think he has picked up some more mares. Take a look." Red moved over. "Don't move it now!"

"Red, he is a beauty! And a good looking band of mares. Are you feeding them," Irene asked.

"None of the herds, which we have released have visited out feeding sites. I think ,they are terrified of our vehicles."

Red stood up and gently drew Irene to him. "Darling, I want to---."

"Please, Red, don't!" Irene laid a finger on Red's lips to stop him. "I think, I know, what you are going to say and please, don't! Not yet. I am not ready to say, yes, and I do not want to say, no. Okay?"

Red took a deep breathe. "Okay, Darling, but I am not giving up!"

"I would be disappointed, if you did," Irene smiled. "Shall we go back, now?"

With the sun well past its zenith, the quads trickled in one at a time. Parker was the last one in. Trace was building himself a giant turkey sandwich with a smile of anticipation on his face.

"Saw those three blue roan yearlings," Walt announced, as he approached the others. "Those little son of a guns almost came up to me!"

"I can't believe, how tame they were," Teresa added.

145

"They were a bit gaunt, though!"

"We climbed Lookout Point and saw the most tremendous view," Irene contributed.

Parker wore a smug grin that he could hardly contain. "Wait until you hear what we did! We trapped another herd! One of the herds we been feeding met us near Echo Canyon and instead of stopping, we just led them into the corral, fed them, and shut the gate! How about that?"

"Hey, great job, Parker and Ben! We are on a roll," Red applauded.

"Any pintos in the bunch," Trace asked hopefully.

"As a matter of fact, pard, there are several! One real nice one," Ben replied

"Boys, it has been a memorial Thanksgiving Day and a real fun day, today, but it is time for me and the girls to get back to the big city." Teresa stopped in front of Walt and gave him a long kiss! "See you Sunday, Handsome."

As Teresa's jeep pulled away, Red looked expectantly at Walt.

"Oh, I forgot to mention, Red," Walt commented casually. "Mister Cooper hired me to assist you in your endeavors. He suggested, no, he insisted that I be your official truck driver for at least four weeks. Until my collar bone is definitely healed." Walt grinned smugly.

"Seriously, Boss, Mister Cooper is really happy with, what you are doing and is hoping that by adding more men, you can accelerate the program. He said to tell you that you could hire one more man, if you need him, and that, since we are starting a full-fledged feeding program, in addition to the trapping, he would move the hay bill out from your budget!"

CHAPTER 25

Red Goes To Phoenix

With three lassos around her neck, pulling in three different directions, the pinto mare was unable to put up much of an argument as Trace slid a hackamore over her head and snubbed her to a hitching post.

"You behave, girl. You and I are going to be good friends," Trace told her.

"Come on, Trace, quite smooth talking her and help us cut these other mares out of here," Ben called from aboard the buckskin gelding he was riding.

In a short while, three fine looking mares were returned to the corral and the hungry culls, including an aging stallion, were loaded into the trailer for a trip to town. Walt gave a wave of his arm, as he drove away!

Parker took his quad, with its load of bales toward Wolf Creek to feed the wild horses ranging near there. Ben and Trace put the pinto between them on a very short rope and rode back to camp. The wild pinto mare fought vigorously for a mile or two, and then settled down to a steady lope. She joined the spare saddle horses in the camp corral. There, she would occupy every spare minute of Trace's time during the coming weeks!

Red's crew had Sunday off, and Walt returned that evening with Micah in tow.

Red had adopted the system of unloading some of the bales and hanging out, until the wild horses overcome their fear of the quad. This had sped up the training of the mustangs, making it possible to lead them into a corral, after only a few times of feeding them!

Red and Micah had driven the quad with the trailer full of bales to the Raidy's Springs area and were greeted by a large group of wild horses. Micah sat on the trailer and doled out a handful of hay at a time, as Red led them all into the large corral there. They broke up several bales of hay and leaving the horses munching contentedly, they closed the entrance and drove on to the Seeps area. There, they hoped to find a couple herds that had never been fed, and they could start the process again!

With the expanded crew and the use of hay to trap and tame the wild herds, a steady stream of culls rolled into town! Walt would frequently make two trips per day. By Christmas, the totals of culls had risen dramatically, and the number of harems out on the range had noticeably thinned!

On the afternoon, before Christmas, the girls gave a repeat performance of the Thanksgiving dinner!

Irene had picked up Beth and the two of them proceeded to unload a card table and four chairs, a nativity scene and a gas floodlight to illuminate it, a large armload of logs, and a stack of pies!

Teresa carried a complete Christmas dinner in her Wrangler and Walt enlisted Ben and Trace to help set things on the old picnic table and card table. Red and Micah arranged the nativity scene, the flood light and several candles.

As dusk crept across the camp, the candles were lit and the small campfire crackled with smoke curling into the still night air.

Red switched on a recorder and the strains of "Silent Night" filled the evening. Red, in a passable baritone, led the group in singing several old Christmas Hymns. He then opened his Bible to Luke, 2, and, with Irene holding a small LED light on the pages, he read the Christmas story of the birth of Christ. When he had finished, he asked a blessing upon their food.

"Dear Father God, it has been a year since we celebrated Your Son's birthday, and it has been a great year for me. The opportunity to celebrate Christmas in Your great outdoors, away from the crowds of Santa Claus lovers is really a good thing! It is almost, as if I can see and hear the multitude of angels proclaiming the virgin birth!

"I want to thank You for a job, which I love and for the circle of friends, which you surrounded me. Bless this food, Lord, and please give a special touch to our evening. Amen!"

Christmas morning was particularly cold and crisp. Everyone was up early and the girls prepared breakfast, while the wranglers loaded down the quads with bales. After breakfast, Trace and Micah volunteered to clean up and tend to the saddle horses. Trace would slip in some time with his pinto mare, which was succumbing, to a diet of hay, grain and love.

Red set the pace by insisting Irene drive and soon, the quads scattered toward the feeding sites with their lady drivers. The sun was warm, but the air was cold so little time was spent with the herds, and the quad were soon back at camp!

Red was startled by his phone ringing, as he climbed from the quad! It was Richard Cooper.

"Sorry to bother you on Christmas Day, Red. I trust you are through with the festivities!"

"No problem, Boss. Hope you have had a good Christmas," Red responded.

"Yes, thank you. Can your crew operate without your presence for a few days?"

"Sure, Boss. They can get along without me. What's up?"

"A friend of mine has an equal position as mine with the BLM in Arizona," Cooper explained. "His name is Roland Langford. He wants to talk with you, regarding, what you are doing here. His office is in Phoenix, and you will take a company car and draw per diem. Let me know, when it is convenient, and I will set up an appointment. Any problem?"

"No. No problem that I can think of, Boss," Red replied. "Could I redo my schedule and get back with you tomorrow?"

"I will be in my office after eight. Call me." Richard Cooper hung up.

The others looked at Red expectantly as he smiled to himself and holstered his phone.

"Don't tell me! You're going to take off and leave all the work to us," Parker exclaimed.

Red just ignored him and addressed Irene. "You are out of school until January, right?"

"Why, yes. January sixth, actually," Irene replied, puzzled.

"I just got orders from the boss to go to Phoenix for a one day meeting! How would you like to go with me and hang out a couple days? Nice weather, heated swimming pool, spa. The works!" Red smiled at the thought of Irene in a swimming suit!

"Oh! I'd love--!" Irene stopped. "Oh, I couldn't! What would people think?"

"Nonsense!" Teresa interrupted. "You simply have separate rooms!" To Red, "of course she will go!"

"I don't know," Irene vacillated.

"It will be great, Irene," Beth chipped in. "Your friends will applaud, and what others think, doesn't matter.

"How about, I call your Dad." Red gave the final argument! "If he says, okay, you go!"

"All right." Irene gave in. "If Dad doesn't object, I will go!"

"When," Red asked.

"Friday," Irene decided. "That will give us the weekend; you can attend your meeting Monday and drive back Tuesday. That is New Year's Eve."

"Pick you up at seven thirty, Friday morning," Red promised.

The drive to Phoenix was long, but uneventful. It was full dark, when they arrived, but Red had reserved rooms at Western Travel Lodge, so their rooms were waiting for them.

CHAPTER 26

A New Job Offer

When Red stepped into Roland Langford's office, he was surprised to see a number of people waiting for him. A stocky, gray-haired man greeted him with outstretched hand.

"You must be Red Iverson. I am Langford. Thank you for coming."

"Yes, I'm Iverson. My pleasure," Red responded.

"You are here, primarily to inform my superior, the head of the State of Arizona sector of the Bureau of Land Management, of your mode of operation, your goals, your accomplishments and your reasoning for adopting this system." Mister Langford informed him and indicated the man behind him. "This is Daren Wooster."

"I don't like the term, superior," Daren Wooster smiled as he extended his hand. "I happen to have more time with the Bureau, than Roland. Would you like some coffee and/or a Danish before you speak?"

At Red's shake of his head, Roland Langford introduced Red to the others and gave him the floor.

"I was not expecting a formal presentation, so I have no formal speech prepared," Red began. "This is, however, a subject dear to my heart and, I believe, I can talk without notes."

This drew a chuckle from his audience.

"My task is to trap the wild horses, one herd at a time, using fenced watering spots, much like the old West system, and leading them into the traps with baled hay in the winter. We cull out the inbred and inferior stock to be sent back for adoption, therein accomplishing two goals, the thinning out of the herds and upgrading them, so that a ready market for quality horses can be tapped, later. There presently exists an overabundance of stock for adoption, because they are not quality horseflesh!"

"Our short term goal is to reduce the number of wild horses in our area from twenty seven hundred to around a thousand. Because the range has been badly over grazed, we also have a feeding program. In the seven months, that we have been operating, we are just under half way to that goal. Long term, I hope to maintain the horses to a sustainable number and by culling out initially, producing top quality animals, which will be in high demand by the public."

"My system also eliminates costly giant drives, which injure horses and excite the ire of the public! Does anyone have any questions?" Red ended.

"Weren't you involved in the big drive in the Muskrat Basin Area of Wyoming?" This from one of the listeners.

"No, I was not involved in the drive. I was in charge of the culling out of the herd, after the drive, and releasing the best of them back to the wilds," Red responded.

"Wasn't there a lot of injuries and dead horses from that operation," the same voice persisted.

"My crew was obliged to put two mustangs out of their misery, and there were thirty-one injured and under a veterinarian's care," Red admitted, "but none of them were injured in the culling and transportation process! We don't know how many were maimed or killed out on the range."

"Does anyone else have questions of Mister Iverson?" Daren Wooster took charge of the meeting and after a short pause. "Mister Iverson, your words only reinforce, what I have gleaned from Richard Cooper and other sources. The Bureau has always been under pressure from certain areas of the public, because of misunderstandings and lack of knowledge from some segments of the animal lovers. Now we are being under attack from certain members of Congress,

---

152

especially the Arizona District."

"The Bureau is in the process of setting up a department for the sole purpose of managing the wild horses of this State," he continued. "We would look favorably on an application from you, to head that department!"

Mister Wooster looked expectantly at Red, who wore a look of utter surprise!

There was a long pause while Red collected his thoughts!

"I am sure you need time to think this over," Mister Wooster finally said,

"No! It's not that," Red responded decisively. "It is a wonderful opportunity, and I would jump at the chance to enhance the program of wild horse management. It is only that I encouraged my employer, Mister Cooper to try out my system. He kind of stuck his neck out, and I would be remiss to drop out now, in the middle of the program. We need a couple more years to prove its worth. I am deeply honored, however, for your offer!"

"There is a substantial increase in salary," Roland Langford mentioned, "perhaps--."

Red cut him off with a wave of his hand.

"If you all are interested, I could recommend a man, who, I believe, is just as capable as I am. I would need his permission, before I mention his name," Red offered.

"Yes," Daren Wooster responded immediately. "Frankly, we had no other choices. I was convinced, you would accept the position. I do, however, commend your loyalty to Richard. Please submit your recommendations as soon as possible."

Red left the meeting with mixed emotions! Not that he had any doubts or regrets about his decision, but he wondered, how Irene would react. He had made no effort to hide his intention to offer marriage to her, when she would allow it. A change in jobs would definitely improve his position!

Half way to the motel, his cell phone jingled! Red pulled over to the curb before answering!

"Red, are you there? This is George Harris, Happy New Year!"

"George! The same to you! Good to hear from you. What's going on?"

"You will never guess where I am at! Phoenix! Mister Wagner advanced me some money and I have moved my mother here into a nice apartment. She looks years younger and is excited about getting her high school diploma." George was bubbling over. "I just had to tell you!"

"Hey, George! I am in Phoenix also. Could we get together for lunch or something? It would be great to see you," Red responded. "I am at the Western Travel Lodge at the edge of town. On the corner of Highway Seventeen and One Oh One. They have a nice restaurant."

"Deal! Meet you at eleven forty-five. Gotta go!" George rang off.

Although Irene had, so far, rebuffed Red's efforts to propose marriage, he had a feeling that she would be unhappy with his decision to reject the job offer from the Arizona BLM. In spite of that, he decided to tell her the whole story, when he returned to the motel!

"Oh, Red, I can't believe you could turn down such a magnificent promotion! We, er, you could have a nice house or an apartment in town instead of living in a tent. And the money, you would have to get a substantial raise in salary. Oh, Red! You would be the head of a department. You would be somebody, not just a wildhorse hunter!"

The glow that possessed Red as he related the compliment that he had been paid, slowly faded and his face turned to stone.

"Just a wildhorse hunter," he repeated as he rose to his feet.

The significance of, what she had just said slowly dawned on Irene, as she saw the transformation.

"Red! I didn't mean that!" She flew to his side. "Oh please forgive me! I was angry!" She tugged at his arm imploringly. "Please, God, help me take those words back!"

Red gently removed her hand from his arm and

stepped away from her.

"I am meeting George Harris for lunch shortly. Pack your things, we will leave for home right after." Red walked to the door, leaving the girl sobbing behind him.

As Red sat in a booth at the restaurant, the words kept repeating themselves in his mind, "just a wildhorse hunter, just a wildhorse hunter"! He ordered a cup of coffee, as he waited for George to arrive, striving to turn his mind toward his new friend, and what he must want to talk to him about. Fortunately, George was a bit early and spotted Red immediately.

"Red, it is good to see you." George rushed over to Red's booth.

"Just can't thank you enough for getting me in touch with Mister Wagner," George continued, as Red rose to greet him.

"You are more than welcome, George," Red replied. "You are looking fine and a little sunburned for an Easterner in January."

Seated now, "Mom's apartment complex has a pool. I have been catching some sun rays," George admitted. "Need to show off a bit, when I get back to school! Have you ordered?"

"Nope. Waiting for you, but we can now," Red motioned to the waitress.

Red was not good at hiding his feelings and, when their orders were taken, George sat back and examined his friend.

"Something is the matter, Red. Is there anything I can do?"

"No, George. Just had a little tiff with my girlfriend," Red grinned unconvincingly. "This meeting is about you. We'll be fine!"

"Well," George commenced, a little reluctantly. "I have always been a little curious about my father. I guess most any boy would be. Mom will not talk about him at all. I ask Mister Wagner about trying to find him. He said, as a general rule, searches by the off- spring of broken marriages tend to reveal circumstances, which are better off not uncovered!"

"Red, what was he trying to tell me? That I shouldn't try to find my father? Does he know something about my father and me? Do you know something about my father, Red?"

"What? Why would you ask me that?" Red stared at his friend, in shock.

"Well, it's just-. What would you do in my place, Red," George asked.

The food arrived at that moment and Red breathed a sigh of relief. A couple minutes to think of the correct reply.

The food stood untouched, as George awaited Red's answer.

"George, I really don't think I can give an honest answer to that. One thing I know though. When you open an unfamiliar door, you must be prepared to face what is on the other side! There could be a lion or a lamb. Great news or bad news. It is a fifty-fifty proposition. Your father could be a great statesman or a well-known minister. On the other hand, he could be serving twenty years in prison for robbing an old woman. How much is your curiosity worth?" Red picked up his fork. "Would you like to say grace?"

"Lord, give me wisdom regarding my dilemma and bless this food. Keep Your hand on my friend as he travels back to Wyoming. Amen! Thanks, Red. That was good counsel. I have to decide for myself." George settled the napkin in his lap and began to eat.

After the goodbyes, Red wended his way reluctantly back to the motel room. The trip back to Wyoming was not going to be pleasant!

Unlike the trip down to Phoenix, which had been full of laughter, singing and even some hand holding, the return trip was ice cold and full of silence!

Irene made several attempts at conversation, only to be met with grunts or nothing at all! Red was not going to communicate. They made stops for gas and several times, Red purchased food and drinks. Knowing that he would be driving all night, Red fortified himself with a thermos full of black coffee. A CD played endlessly. It was a long journey!

From midnight on, Irene slept fitfully, awakening when they entered the Laramie city limits. Dawn was breaking.

Red stopped at Irene's apartment and silently unloaded Irene's luggage and carried them to her door. With a last look at her stricken face, he drove way. He still had one hundred miles to drive.

CHAPTER 27

Promoted

Red elected to stop at a fast food place to shave, clean up and gulp down a breakfast sandwich before appearing at Richard Cooper's office. He couldn't erase the ravages of the al-night drive completely from his face, but it was an improvement.

"You are back early," was Mister Cooper's comment when Red stepped into his office. "I thought you would spend a couple more days. Wasn't it good weather there?"

"Weather was fine, Boss. I was finished with the meeting and thought I should get back to the horses," Red replied, somewhat unconvincingly.

"Tell me about your meeting."

"It wasn't quite like I expected, Boss. Mister Langford actually just introduced me to a Daren Wooster. He is the head of the Arizona branch of the BLM." Red commenced.

"I know Daren," Richard Cooper inserted, "go ahead."

"Well, I explained, how we operated and our goals and gave him a progress report." Here, Red hesitated.

Richard Cooper waited, without comment.

"They are opening up a new department for the sole purpose of managing the wild horses in all the Arizona

---

158

territory," Red finally blurted out. "They offered me the job of heading that department!"

"And you accepted, of course." Richard Cooper leaned forward encouragingly.

"Well, no, Boss. I didn't." Red was beginning to think that he had made a mistake.

"Why not," Mister Cooper persisted.

"Mister Cooper," Red began a bit stiffly. "I committed to do a job. I feel obligated to stay with you, until my idea has been proven to be a good one."

There was a short pause while Richard Cooper studied his employee. Then he picked up a paper from his desk and handed it to Red.

"Read this!"

The paper contained a request from Richard Cooper to the head of BLM, asking to establish a central department to be totally responsible for the numerous wild horse herds in Wyoming. I went on to list supporting arguments for such a department and some disadvantages. Underneath was a handwritten note from the BLM Director.

"Excellent idea. Pick out a man to run it, and help him make out a budget, and a Standard Operating Procedures paper. Send them to me ASAP. It will take a couple of weeks to get final approval, but consider it a done deal."

Wordlessly, Red returned the paper.

"Arizona isn't the only one to think of that," Richard Cooper grunted. "Are you going to turn this job down, also?"

"No, Boss." For the first time since Red had entered the office, he began to smile. "If you think that I can handle it, I'll take the job!"

Richard Cooper nodded and stood up. Red, thinking the meeting was over started to stand, also. He was waved back to his seat, as his boss walked to the window and looked out. Nothing was said for a full minute, and then he turned back to Red and leaned on the windowsill.

"I don't often mix with my people's personal affairs, but you looked like a whipped pup, when you walked into my office and I don't mean, because you drove all night. A department head must have his private life in order, especially starting a new department. There is a lot of stress involved! So, I am asking. Is your private life in order?"

Red shrunk a little under the steady gaze of his boss!

"No, Boss, I can't say that it is," he paused to gather his thoughts. "I thought everything was going great until yesterday. You know she drove down to Phoenix with me." His boss nodded for him to continue. "We had a great weekend. Oh, she had her own room, but we laid around the pool, ate out at fancy restaurants and just enjoyed each other. Well, I told her about the job offer and that I had turned them down. I knew she wouldn't be too happy about it, but she called me just a wildhorse hunter and somehow, the way she said it, made it sound like, I was just one step lower than a pimp! We drove back fifteen hours without talking!" Red raised his hands in a gesture of surrender.

"So, you are all through with her, now?"

"I don't know, Boss. I love doing what I am doing. Hunting wild horses never seemed like a little thing to me. I have never been happier in my whole life." Red stood up and paced around his chair. "But I don't want to let her go, I love her!"

"Then go tell her that!"

"What?" Red stared at his boss in amazement.

"Red, what did you expect? That she would marry you, move into your tent with the other two guys, and live happily ever after? Face it, Red. As much fun as you were having running around in the desert, trapping wild horses, it was and is a dead end job. There are no promotions in that billet. A woman needs a home and her man to come back to it every night. Don't let a remark that Irene said in anger, ruin a good thing. Climb back in my company car, go back to Laramie, and settle this thing! Then come and see me, and we will get this new department running!"

Richard Cooper went back to his desk and sat down. Their meeting was over and Red stumbled from the office.

Almost in a daze, Red returned to the sedan, which he had been driving the last seventeen hours.

"Move into a tent! Dead end job! Woman needs a home!" These words echoed in his brain.

He rolled down the window to let the near freezing

wind clear his mind.

"What a fool I am! How could I talk of marriage with no money, no home and no future? I do have a dead end job. I am just a wildhorse hunter. She was right! Will she forgive me?"

His face cleared and began to glow.

"But it is all different now! I will be a department head, a director. I can afford a nice home or an apartment. I can make her proud of me!"

The miles sped by, as he pushed the car well past the speed limit. He fumbled for his cell phone and pressed the speed dial button.

"You have reached Irene Fallon. I am having a wonderful day and hope you are also. Please leave your name and phone number, so I can return your call. Good bye,"

"Irene, darling! I will be there in about an hour. Please wait for me. I love you!" Red slipped his phone back in to his pocket. "Please, God, let her be home!"

Red could hear running footsteps, almost before he removed his hand from the doorbell. The door burst open and hands pulled him inside!

"Praise God, you've come back! Thank You, Lord, for answering my prayers! Oh, Red, forgive me. I love you! I didn't mean what I said. I was angry! Please marry me; we could set up another tent. I'd go anywhere with you. I am proud of my wildhorse hunter!" Tears were streaming down Irene's cheeks. Her hands fluttered around Red's face.

He stopped the torrent of words pouring out of her the only way he knew. He crushed her in his arms and closed her lips with his lips! Slowly she relaxed and he released her very slightly

"Oh, Red! I thought you were gone forever!" Her words were muffled as her head was buried in his coat.

"Ssh, Darling. You were right. As much as I enjoyed my work, I was just a wildhorse hunter with no future." Red took a deep breath. "I do want to marry you, and you won't have to live in a tent. Well, maybe just for our honeymoon." Red held her away from him, so he could see her face. A big grin spread over his face.

"You see. The Wyoming BLM has offered me the same job. I will be the new head of the Department of Wild Horse Preservation over the Wyoming area! You will have a home of your own, and I will be your slave!"

The pleased look on Irene's face did not come up to Red's expectations.

"I'm glad, Darling, but where we live doesn't seem quite as important, as it did ,and I will be proud of you, no matter what your job is." Her face was back in his coat again.

Red's grin faded into a look of resignation. Who could understand a woman?

CHAPTER 28

Good News

It was a sheepish wrangler, who stood before Richard Cooper, turning his Stetson around and around in his hands.

"Well?" Richard Cooper was not one to waste words."

"I, ah, can report that my private life is in order, Mister Cooper." Red suddenly grinned. "We are going to get married, Boss."

"Good. The Bureau doesn't like unmarried directors. They tend to be unstable. You have several weeks to train a successor. Who will that be?" Richard Cooper sat with pencil poised.

"Parker should be fine, Boss. He has been active in most all the decisions to date," Red replied without hesitation.

"Parker it is. He brought in two loads of horses, while you were gone. Seems to be on top of it. He will take over March first. You will return here, and we will hash out a budget and SOP, plus many other details. Anything else?"

"Yes, there is, Boss. I promised Mister Wooster that I would recommend someone to head up his department. I need to talk to Walt first, but I think he would be right for the job," Red responded.

"Do we have a resume on him?"

"No," Red admitted. Assuming he will be interested, I'll send him in to write something up. Might include that article Teresa Castell wrote up on him for the Laramie paper. That should do it," Red added with a grin.

Richard Cooper looked at Red with his head cocked to one side a bit.

"I know you were joking, but it is a good idea and great publicity. I will contact Miss Castell and get a copy to Daren! Call me and/or send Walt in to see me, and I will get a letter off to Daren. Now! You are to check into a motel and get some sleep, before you go back to base camp. That is an order!"

Richard Cooper stood up. The meeting was over.

Obedient to his boss's direction, Red crashed into a motel bed in the middle of the afternoon. As a result, he was wide awake at four o'clock in the following morning. Not bothering to shave or have breakfast, he drove directly to base camp. It was still dark, and the camp was still asleep. Red lit the stove and started the coffee. Then, he mixed up some pancakes, sliced some ham and beat some eggs for an omelet. He would have a nice surprise for his sleeping crew.

It was a still, frosty morning and the aroma of coffee and frying ham drifted over the sleepers as the dawn commenced to break. Here and there, a body groaned, partially awake and turned over.

Red grabbed a pan and commenced to beat on it. "Stampede! Grab your horses and head for the hills!"

Instant bedlam reigned as the men bolted from their bedrolls. Two pistols appeared, as the men grabbed for their boots!

One of them coolly sat up and looked around him.

"Head for the hills? Come on, Red. You can do better than that." Walt grinned as he surveyed the chaos around him.

"Would you believe, head for the breakfast table," Red grinned back at him. "Breakfast in ten minutes," he continued in a louder voice.

"Ah, Red! I was having this great dream," Parker grumbled as he headed for the stream to wash. "Now I forgot what it was!"

"Pretty dang funny," was Micah's contribution. He always woke in a surly mood.

"That coffee smells great! Welcome back, Boss. How was your trip?" Ben reached for the coffee pot, the first one back from washing up.

"Hey, Ben. Pour me a cup while you're at it." Trace was already seated at the table and reaching for the pancakes.

With everyone seated, Red asked the blessing over the food, and the stack of pancakes speedily began to disappear.

Red finished first and pushed his plate away.

"You guys are getting a new boss!"

Forks stopped in mid-air! Silence reigned for half a minute, as they stared at him, waiting for Red to elaborate.

"What are you saying, Red," Parker finally got out.

Red grinned at the consternation, he was creating. "Actually, Parker. You are going to be the new boss!"

At that, everybody tried to talk at once, until Red held up his hands. After everyone was quiet, he continued.

"The BLM is creating a new Department of Wild Horse Preservation, and I am to be the department head of the Wyoming branch!"

A series of exclamations echoed around the table, as the men expressed their good wishes.

"So you are going to be riding a desk, Red?" Parker was dumbfounded! "And I got to boss these clowns?"

"Well, you wouldn't expect me to bring my wife out here to live in a tent, would you?" Red ask the question with a straight face.

"Whoopee! You son-of-a-gun! You finally popped the question to Irene!" Walt hopped up from his seat and came around the table to shake Red's hand.

"If you got anymore bombshells to drop on us, Boss, would you kindly wait, until I have finished my breakfast," was Trace's contribution, as he speared another pancake.

Breakfast was resumed and Red began to gather up the dirty dishes. Walt finished and handed his plate to Red.

"Hey, Buddy, how about giving me a hand," Red asked, as he accepted Walt's dirty plate.

Walt nodded and picked up the empty pancake platter.

"Bring your coffee with you," Red called over his shoulder.

Walt obediently grabbed he cup, and followed Red, as he refilled his coffee cup. Red led the way over to a rock, out of earshot from the others.

"What do you think of my new job, Walt?"

"Gee, Boss, I think it's great. You can improve the wild horse program all over the State," Walt waxed enthusiasm.

"Walt, there is an opening for the same billet in Arizona. Would you be interested?"

Walt looked over at Red with a startled look.

"You mean it, Boss?"

"We get to start with a clean sheet. Write our own procedures. Just have to keep the media off our boss's back, and make the animal lovers happy. Gonna be a bunch of paper work, but we can get out in the field, too. We could trade data; it is a great opportunity for both of us. I promised I would let them know ASAP. What do you think, Walt?" Red leaned back and studied his friend.

The stunned look on Walt's face was replaced by a sort of glow!

"If you think I can handle it, Red, I'll do it!" Walt place an arm on Red's shoulder. "And thanks, pard."

"You will be making about four times the wages that I have been paying you, Walt. Maybe enough to get married on," Red mentioned slyly.

They were interrupted by Parker's shout. "We got a herd of horses over at Wolf Creek to take care of, unless you all are going to chat all morning!"

Leave me a Quad," Red shouted back. "I will join you shortly. Walt's riding into town."

Parker nodded and him and the others climbed into the truck and drove away.

"I got to tell Teresa," Walt exclaimed, as Red turned back to him.

"No. It's only ninety percent sure," Red contradicted. "First, you go see Mister Cooper and fill out a job application.   He will send it with his letter of recommendation to the Arizona Branch. Daren Wooster, of the Arizona BLM, will probably want an interview. When it is all set, then you call Teresa!"

CHAPTER 29

Director of Wild Horse Preservation

It took only a couple of days before Richard Cooper called Red with the news that he had been appointed to the director position.

The days ahead were full of planning for Red and Walt, whom Red had enlisted to aid him on a short time basis. They both were counting on Walt's getting the equal appointment from the Arizona BLM.

Uncertain, if he would be assigned a base, Red begged a small office from Richard Cooper and hunted up a map of the several Wild Horse Management Areas, referred to as HMAs.

Wyoming has sixteen HMAs, managed by five field offices. Red had met two of the Field Directors, his ex-boss controlled the Rawlins office and J.B. Honeycutt, of the Lander's office. He determined to meet the others before completing the Standard Operating Procedure (SOP) for his position. Besides a social call, he needed to know the conditions of both the horses and the winter grazing. Also, each HMA would have its own unique problems to work around. He decided to establish a billet in each of the field offices to be responsible to their assigned HMAs.

"I'll start with the Lander's area, where I think Charlie Simmons had been hired," he remarked to Walt.

"Could you get a hold of J.B. Honeycutt and get a contact number for Charlie?"

Red flipped through the office phone book and gave him the number, while he continued to copy down the Director's names and phone numbers for the Cody, Worland and Rock Springs Field Offices.

Walt handed Red a scrap of paper. "Charlie's cell phone".

Red accepted the paper and handed Walt his in return.

"Would you call these guys and explain, who we are and get a convenient time to drop in on them next week? I'll need two days each at Cody and Worland so try to get them adjacent days. It's a long way up there!"

Red carefully dialed the phone number, which Walt had given him. A voice at the other end answered, "Charlie Simmons."

"Charlie, this is Red Iverson. I am wondering, how you are doing in your new job."

"Hi, Red. Things are going great. Can't thank you enough for getting me this job. I love what I am doing."

"I just gave J.B. your name, Charlie. You got the job on your own merits. I have a new job now, also. I am the director of a new branch of BLM. I am responsible for the wild horse herds in all of Wyoming," Red declared. "I will be establishing the same thing that you are doing in each of the Field Offices."

"Wow! You got your work cut out for you, Red! Wishing you good luck with it," Charlie responded. "You remember, Slim Well, he is helping me. Using some of the fencing from the big drive, we fenced in several of the water holes that the wild ones like and have been feeding several of the herds. Don't have much of a budget for hay, so can't do much there, although grazing is pretty sparse. Located a couple harems that avoided the big round-up and trapped them with hay. One stud was old and most of the mares were culls. That's about it. Next year the winter grazing should be better with that big bunch of culls gone, which you cut out."

"Sounds like you have a handle on it, Charlie. I plan to be over to see you and J.B. next week, if things work out.

See you then." Red rang off.

"Both of the directors are keeping the first part of next week open for you," Walt stated, when Red had shut up his phone. "Both seemed glad to get rid of the wild horse problem and are anxious to see you."

The following day was Friday and Red was looking forward to a weekend away from the desk and telephone and a couple of days with Irene.

Walt accepted a call from Darin Wooster in Arizona, requesting an interview with him regarding the position of Director of Wild Horse Preservation. Ignoring Red's advice about telling Teresa about it, he persuaded her to accompany him to Phoenix for the weekend prior to Monday's interview.

Monday morning, Red wanted an early start. It would take about five hours to drive to Worland. The lady at the café, where he had breakfast, obligingly packed a couple of sandwiches and some chips for his lunch and fortified with a thermos of coffee, two canteens of water, he set out. As an afterthought, he tossed a couple of blankets in the company SUV.

He passed the Lander's field office about nine-thirty and considered stopping, briefly, but decided to push on.

"Can always catch them later," he mumbled to himself.

He slipped in a disc of religious music by the Gathers and sat back to enjoy the next three hour's drive. It was a clear day and the landscape picturesque.

After an hour of low foothills and the road leveled out, bordering the Indian Reservation, he espied far ahead, what appeared to be an animal on the roadside. As he approached, it developed that a horse was plodding toward him. Red slowed the vehicle for a closer look.

"Odd looking saddle! It's riding way forward! No! The back cinch is broken and dragging. The rider must have roped something and the cinch gave away! But where is the rider?"

Red stopped the vehicle and stepped out.

"Whoa, boy,' he called to the little mouse colored

mustang as he slowly approached him.

The mustang obediently stopped, obviously tired and hurt. He stood quietly while Red walked around him.

"Dirt and sand ground into dried sweat! This animal took a fall. Oh, oh! Gash on his back leg! I'll need some powder from my first-aid kit. Reckon his rider is back there hurt!"

Red loosened the saddle and set it on straight, and pulled out a long branch from a shrub that was under it. Hurriedly he washed and dressed the wound and tied one canteen to the saddle horn. After a second's reflection, he removed a blanket from the back seat and threw it over the saddle. Lastly, before setting out he poured the water from his second canteen into his hat and offered it to the horse. It drank greedily.

"I'm sorry, little horse, to make you walk back, but I might need you," he told the little mustang, and picking up the reins, he started back-trailing. "Hope these tracks don't peter out before I find the rider!"

The mustang, refreshed by his hat full of water and encouraged by the human companionship, moved along easily enough. Red was able to trot part of the time on the road pavement, while the horse jogged on the softer soil adjoining.

The tracks followed along the roadway for about a quarter mile, before dropping into a gully, where it struck a beaten trail and dodged abruptly under a bridge in the main highway. The mustang's tracks were still easily discernable, but, Red, concerned about the welfare of the missing rider, elected to mount up and ride the mustang to save time.

"Sorry, partner. I know you are tired, but your master must be lying out here somewhere, needing help. You got to hang in there a while longer."

Now moving at a fast trot, they moved steadily west into the Indian Reservation. Suddenly, Red pulled back on the reins and slapped his forehead.

"You klutz! Your phone!" He checked the reception. "Two bars! I'll call for help. So it's a false alarm! Big deal! I'll call nine-one-one now. Maybe they will send a chopper out. Probably would need to come from Laramie and take an hour or so to get here."

The emergency operator agreed to send a helicopter from Laramie after locating him by his cell phone towers. She also offered to send a four-wheel emergency ground vehicle from Landers to help Red search, which he accepted.

"They will find my white Bureau of Land Management sedan, parked along the highway, just as they approach the Indian Reservation. I am on a trail a quarter mile north of there, heading west on horseback," Red told her. "I am back tracking the mustang, he was riding."

Red's watch told him that it was straight up noon, and hunger pangs were reminding him that it had been a long time since breakfast. He stopped and dismounted, deciding to walk a while to rest the mustang and eat a sandwich.

Having washed the food down with a swig from the canteen, Red had just remounted when the tracks abruptly turned off the main trail, and headed toward the foothills. They appeared to be heading for a large clump of trees some two or three miles to the southwest.

The mustang seemed to pick up the pace, indicating that there was water up ahead and Red sensed that he was getting close to his destination. A mile passed, as Red anxiously surveyed the surrounding. It could be easy to miss a body.

"He can't be lying very far from the horse tracks," he reassured himself.

He checked his cell phone again. No reception! Regretfully, he replaced his phone.

"So much for our modern electronic devices! Fine for social chit chat, but just another piece of junk, when you really need it!"

Suddenly, the mustang stopped of its own volition. Red stared at the tracks. They were deep and erratic! The animal had struggled to its feet, here! A second set of horse track led off to the right, deep and running!

"Good grief! A big horse from the size of those prints! What!!? He was pulling the mustang! That big horse was pulling our little mustang like a sled, sideways. Two, three hundred yards! I got it! That is how the saddle cinch broke; the mustang was being pulled by the saddlehorn! The rope must have broken here. Here's where he fell, ahh!"

Red was out of the saddle like a flash and kneeling beside the prostrate form, lying in the sand! It was just a boy!

"Where are you hurting, Son," Red asked.

"Thank God! Some-body came--, sent Smokey home--, prayin someone—would come," the boy whispered brokenly, a tear trickled down one filthy cheek. He was breathing in short choppy breaths.

Red ran back to the mustang for his canteen and gently raised the boy's head and trickled some water into his mouth.

"You are going to be all right, Son. Help is on its way," Red tried to assure him. "Where are you hurting?"

"Think- have broken rib. Can't feel legs. Afraid of back-," the eyes looked up pleading. "Please- see-if back-broken!"

"I don't want to move you, Son. I could hurt you more," Red demurred.

"Name- Bucky. Please-, don't want- to live- if- back broke. Please lift- me."

Unable to deny the pleading in those dark eyes, Red slid his arm under the boy's shoulder and gently raised him to a half-sitting position.

Bucky stifled a cry of pain and clutched his ribs, but a smile shone briefly on his face.

"Thank you, Mister. Back- is- okay! Could I- have- more- water?"

Holding the boy with one arm, Red placed the canteen to his lips, and the boy swallowed several times. Carefully, Red eased the boy back on the sand and slipped out of his coat, which he placed under the boy's head. Then, returning to the mustang, he secured the blanket and used it to cover the boy.

"Bucky, my name is Red. I am expecting a helicopter before long and I need to gather some firewood to make some smoke, so they can find us. Will you be okay, while I leave you for a bit?"

"I'll- be okay- Mister- Red. Feel- better- now."

Hurriedly, Red scurried around, picking up a twig

here and a branch there, until he had an armload. He dumped it a hundred feet from, where the boy lay and repeated the action three times. He stacked the pile with small twigs at the bottom over a wad of paper from his notebook. Lastly, he cut some green branches from some growing shrubs and placed them on the top of his pile of firewood.

"That ought to do it," he called out to Bucky and checked his cigarette lighter for reliability.

Satisfied that he would be able to attract the attention of the helicopter crew, if they got close, he returned to Bucky's side.

"Mister- Red. Is Smokey- okay?" The boy was holding an arm tightly against his chest.

"He is tired, dirty and thirsty and has a cut on his back leg. It appears that he was pretty badly used, Bucky, but I think, he is all right," Red replied. "How old are you, Bucky?"

"I'm- almost fourteen-, Mister Red-, but I did- an awful- dumb thing. Was- giving Smokey- a drink- at the Springs,- when- I heard- horses coming. It- was that- sorrel stud- with his herd- of wild- horses. I hid- behind the- trees, and- they came right- on. I had seen- the sorrel- many times and- lot of- guys have- tried to catch- him, but- he is fast- as the wind. I- was down wind,- and he didn't- smell or see- me and walked- right into- my rope."

"Poor Smokey- couldn't hold- him, and he- dragged us- all over- until Smokey- fell. Reckon I- was out- for a spell,- cause they- were gone, when- I woke."

"Don't talk anymore, Bucky. I know it is hurting you," Red hushed him. "Try and--."

Bucky interrupted by raising his hand. "Hear plane!"

Red jumped to his feet and searched the sky, as the distinctive "whop, whop" of a helicopter became audible. He raced over to the pile of firewood, fumbling for his lighter.

The fire caught quickly and black smoke began to rise as the flames reached the green boughs. Anxiously, he again strained his eyes to see the incoming plane.

There it was, just rising above the foothills and heading directly toward them! Red breathed a sigh of relief!

A small dust storm arose, almost putting out Red's

signal fire, as the helicopter settled onto the desert floor. A man hopped out of the right side and trotted toward Red, carrying a small case. The second man, the pilot, followed, with a folded up stretcher. Except for a brief wave of their hands, the men ignored Red and knelt at the boy's side. Red stood over them, but said nothing.

The men spoke among themselves, as they examined the boy.

"Left leg broken just below the knee," one of them muttered.

"Bruise on left side of head," the other said. "Son, is your chest hurting? Move your arm away. I'll try not to hurt you."

His probing fingers produced a small gasp from the boy! "Ah! A broken rib or two! I'm sorry, Son. Going to give you something to stop the pain."

As Bucky relaxed, the first man returned to the helicopter for a set of leg splints. "Let's secure that broken leg first, and then tie up those ribs."

They were loading the boy into the helicopter, when a red emergency vehicle drove up.

"Was tracking you, until we saw the chopper land. Reckon you found the man," the drive remarked.

"A boy, actually," Red replied. "He managed to put his rope on a big wild stallion, and it turned him every way, but loose! He has a busted leg and some ribs, but will be okay."

The driver stepped out and trotted over to look at the boy.

"You taking him to Lander's Medical Center," he asked the pilot.

Upon receiving a nod, he started to turn away and stopped. "Sure do appreciate you men. Reckon you save a lot of lives with that contraption."

The pilot grinned and spun his right hand, indicating he was going to start up. Red and the others ran back to escape the blowing dirt and watched the helicopter rise and head south.

"What shall we do with the pony," Red inquired, when the noise subsided.

"The boy is from the Indian Reservation," the driver answered. "I'll strip the saddle off and drop it off at the village. The mustang will find its way back home. I need to find the kid's folks. I'll drop you at your car, first, though."

"Reckon we owe you, Mister," the second man stated. "Not many folk would take the trouble to look for that kid!"

"You're welcome," Red replied. "Kind of hard to pass up that little mustang. Horses are sort of my business."

At their inquiring looks, Red explained about his work with wild horses. They made introductions and, after stripping the mustang, Smokey, Red climbed into the back of their vehicle, and they drove back to his car.

CHAPTER 30

Red Goes To Work

Red slid behind the wheel of the white departmental sedan with a sigh of relief. He watched the emergency vehicle, which he had emerged from, turn off the highway. The dust cloud from the unpaved road soon obscured the vehicle.

"Headed for the village to find Bucky's folks, I reckon," he told himself, as he dialed a number on his cell phone.

"Could I speak to Mister Malone," he told the feminine voice that answered. "This is Red Iverson. I was supposed to meet him a couple hours ago."

"Mister Malone, I do apologize for standing you up. I ran into an emergency situation on the road there. I am still an hour or more from your place, could we reschedule for the first thing tomorrow morning?"

"Actually, a little Indian boy was seriously hurt, but in no danger, at this point. I will tell you about it tomorrow. Thank you for your patience. Good bye." Thoughtfully, Red replaced the phone and started the car. Still have sixty some miles to go!

Refreshed from a good night's sleep and a bountiful breakfast at a small café near his motel, Red stepped into the outer office of the Worland Field Office. There was no one at the reception desk, but an open door to another office beckoned him. A booming voice emerged from the office.

"That you, Iverson?" A large figure filled the doorway. "Alice doesn't come in until nine. I like to get some things done, while there is no one to bother me." He strode across the room with a big hand outstretched. "Come on in!"

"I'm Buster Malone," he continued, his voice as large as the man. "Coffee is still perking. Let's sit on the sofa and you can tell me, what we are meeting about."

Having passed the ball to Red, Buster Malone uttered not a word as Red explained, what he had been doing for Richard Cooper.

"We apparently impressed the brass in Cheyenne, because, I am instructed to start similar programs in the other field offices," Red finished.

"So you are the new Director of Wild Horses! I'm dang glad to meet you. I was afraid you would be some old grey-haired pencil pusher! From the looks of you, you haven't spent much time indoors lately," Buster rumbled.

Red admitted that riding a desk was not his strong point, and he preferred riding horses to writing about them.

"Up north, here, we don't have the problems of the southern herds. Our forage is better and our herds small," Buster informed him. "Let me give you a tour in my jeep. We can talk, as we drive."

At Red's nod, Buster went to his desk and carefully closed the open Bible lying there, after marking his place. Then, dropping a scribbled note on Alice's desk, he pulled on a sheepskin coat and headed out the door.

"What's this about an Indian boy," Buster shouted above the roar of the jeep engine.

"Well, I just saw this little mustang walking along the highway. The saddle was all screwed up and it was covered with dirt and grime, like it had taken a fall,' Red shouted back. "I stopped and started back tracking it. Found a teenage boy."

Red went on to tell about the stallion and the MedEvac. "The emergency crew were going to find his folks, and take them to the hospital," he ended.

178

"Dang! Lucky you came along! Dang kids are always getting into some trouble!" Buster shook his head.

Thirty minutes later, they sighted the first wild horse herd. The horses didn't appear to be too alarmed by the jeep, but wouldn't allow them to get too close.

"Hey, this stock is in great shape for this time of year. Are you feeding them?" Red was pleasantly surprised.

"Nary a bale. We, Cody and us had a big drive a couple years ago and thinned the herds considerably. Got all the locals upset! They will make sure that we don't do another. What would you like done with this particular herd?"

"You got some nice mares and a good young stud, but here, here and there are some culls, if you want first class herd," Red replied, pointing to several inferior mares. "Also those two year olds are obviously from the stud and there is going to be inbreeding, if you don't move them."

Buster nodded. "Reckon you know, what you're doing. What now?"

"Do you know a couple of reliable young fellows, who know the area and know horses?" Red countered.

"Ho! Ho! Ho!" Buster's laughter boomed out. "This country is full of young bucks, who grew up with horses and have been riding around these parts, since they were big enough to set a saddle. But now, reliable? That's a different story!"

"Oh, come on, Buster. We need a team to trap and cull the herds in this area," Red protested. "They aren't running for Governor! Find a couple men that are married and need or want the money from a steady job. They could spend a couple weeks with my old crew, learning how to put that aluminum fencing together and the systems, which we have perfected for trapping and transporting wild horses. I could send someone up from the Rawlins' area, but I would prefer hiring local talent. The team will be responsible for both Worland and Cody's wild herds as the BLM records you with a couple hundred each, and that needs to be reduced to about two-thirds that many."

"I reckon I can find a couple of acceptable young

179

bucks," Buster was serious now. "Fact is, Alice, my receptionist is engaged to a good candidate. I'll talk to him. You want to see more horse herds?"

"Yes, I would, if it won't take too long," Red replied. "Thought I would drive on to Cody this evening."

"Plenty of time, I'll call Ted Strunk and let him know that you want to see him tomorrow morning." Buster swung the jeep off the main trail. "Generally find a bunch in this little canyon. Good grazing and water."

Buster was correct in that a bay stallion met them near the mouth of the canyon with about twenty some mares and two more herds were watering inside the box canyon with the studs watching each other closely, that no wife stealing would occur! The horses were generally in better condition than the horses in the Rawlins area.

"Good spot for a wild horse trap," Red remarked. "Wouldn't take much fencing with those steep walls, and it has real easy access for the truck and trailer."

Back at Buster's office, Red met Alice. She was an attractive young lady, barely out of her teens. She wore a bright red blouse and white scarf, which set, off her dusky skin to a good advantage. Buster asked about her fiancée, Bud, and brought up the subject of employing him.

"Oh, Mister Malone, that would be super!" Alice's face turned radiant. "Bud won't let me name a wedding date, until he has a steady job!"

Red chuckled at her enthusiasm. "Well, we will have to work on that. Have him fill out a job application and send it to me." Red gave her an e-mail address. "If it looks good, he will have to drive down to Rawlins for an interview. If he has a reliable buddy that needs a job, have him apply also. We need two men."

Red thanked Buster Malone for his time, wished Alice, Bud the very best, and left the office. It was well past lunchtime, so he stopped at a local café before heading north for Cody.

Ted Strunk was well passed middle age. Rather small in stature with a soft voice, he acknowledged that he had only held the post of Director for about eighteen months. He seemed relieved to have the wild horse project out of his hands. He drove Red out to the McCullough Peaks, but seemed oblivious to the beauty that surrounded them.

They visited several horse herds and Red found the situation similar to the Worland's herds. They were back at The Cody field office by noon and Red explained about the team of horse trappers.

"Your only part will be to contact the one's holding the culls so they can pick them up as soon as the team brings them in," he instructed Mister Strunk.

His work here was finished so Red grabbed a quick lunch and headed south.

"Think I'll just drive to Landers and catch a motel there. Want to see how young Bucky is doing. He must still be in the hospital. I can still be home by tomorrow night."

Red was at the reception desk of the Landers' Medical Center at eight o'clock the next morning. He smiled at the grey haired "pink lady" that greeted him.

"I'm looking for an Indian lad about fourteen. His name is Bucky, I don't know his last name. He came in Monday with broken ribs and left arm." Red was a little embarrassed. "That's all I can tell you."

"Oh, dear! That would be Bucky Blackfox. And you must be Mister Red! He has been looking for you, since the hour that they flew him here." The lady smiled happily. "He is on the second floor, room number two eleven. His parents spent the night with him. They will be anxious to meet you, too."

The door to room two-eleven was half-open, when Red arrived. He pushed it open, quietly and looked in.

"It's Mister Red," a voice cried from the hospital bed in the right side of the room. "I knew you would come."

"Hi, Bucky! How are you doing?" Red advanced into the room and stopped at Bucky's side. He clasp the eager right hand of the boy.

"I'm doing okay, Mister Red. I'm going to get well," the boy replied hopefully.

"Of course, you are. What's a couple broken bones to

181

a tough Indian boy? You look like a cocoon about to turn into a butterfly." Red grinned at the bandages around Bucky's chest and the elevated leg, covered with a cast.

The boy started to laugh, but caught himself as a stab of pain from the broken ribs hit him.

The boy's parent stood up. They had been sitting on the other bed. They were both sturdily built of medium height and about thirty-five to forty years old.

"I am Thomas Blackfox, Bucky's dad. This is his mother, Maria. We are most grateful for you coming to the rescue of our son!" The man advanced and held out a hand.

"Oh yes, Mister Red. We were so worried and so relieved, when those men came and told us that he was safe and on his way to the hospital. I don't know what we are going to do with him! He is always getting into some kind of predicament!" Maria grasp Red's hand in both of hers.

"Please, call me Red. My name is Red Iverson and I work for the Bureau of Land Management. I am happy that I happened by. Smoky would have gotten home, if I hadn't discovered him, but it was a lot faster this way. The Lord looks after our kids." Red responded.

"The doctor tells us that he may have gotten pneumonia, if he had laid out overnight," Maria insisted.

"Mister Red saved my life," Bucky averred, as if that settled the matter.

"If that is so, I'm glad!" Red grinned and ruffled the boy's hair.

"You said that you work for the BLM," Thomas asked hesitantly. "I have been out of work for almost a year. Is there anything available?"

"You could try contacting Charlie Simmons at the Landers Field Office," Red replied after a moment's thought. "He is in charge of their horse herds and has a big territory. I am going to try to find him this afternoon. I'll mention you."

"I have to leave now, Bucky." Red gave Bucky's hair another swipe. "Oh! I almost forgot!"

Red stepped back to the doorway, where he had dropped a bag. He reached in and removed a new lariat. He came back to Bucky's bed and dropped it on the bed next to the boy.

"Figured you would need a new lasso since your old one is running around on the desert around the neck of that big stallion." Red chuckled at the surprise and pleasure that flashed across the boy's face.

"Aw, thanks, Mister Red," the boy burst out as he fingered the rope with his good hand. "It even has a metal honda instead of a braided loop! That's great, Mister Red!"

Maria Blackfox followed Red to the door.

"You're a nice man, Red." She gave him a quick hug. "That was real thoughtful."

On the way to his car, Red thumbed through his phone for Charlie Simmons' number. He got into his car before dialing as a cold wind was blowing, as if a storm was brewing.

"Hi Charlie. I'm in Landers, passing through. Thought I would look you up."

"Hi, Red, actually, I'm in J.B.s office as we speak. Why don't you come on over?"

"On my way, Charlie."

J.B. met Red with a big smile and an outstretched hand.

"Congratulations on your promotion, Red. It is a good thing for the department and for the wild life in Wyoming. Frankly, I am amazed at the burst of intelligence from our bosses!"

"Thank you, J.B. I'll do my best for the wild horse herds." Red was a little embarrassed.

"What brings you to Landers, Red," J.B. inquired.

"Just on my way back from visiting the Worland and Cody Field Offices. I wanted to look over the grazing and meet the directors. I also intend to set up teams, such as Charlie has, to control and improve the wild horse herds," Red explained. "I stopped at the hospital to see Bucky, a little Indian boy, who got hurt trying to rope a wild stallion."

"Bucky? That wouldn't be Bucky Blackfox," Charlie interjected.

"That's him," Red replied, surprised. "Do you know him?"

"Everybody around here knows Bucky and Smokey!"

Charlie chuckled. "He has a way of getting into scrapes! What did he do this time?"

"As I understand it, Bucky was watering Smokey at this spring, when he heard horses coming and hid. Seems this wild stallion stops right next to them for a drink and Bucky drops a noose on him," Red explained. "The stallion, being twice the size of Smokey, took off across the desert, just barely slowed down by the kid on his pony. Pretty soon, Smokey fell and dumped off Bucky. The rope broke, luckily, and I found Smokey headed down the road for home. We backed tracked him and found Bucky with a broken leg and ribs and the paramedics flew him into the Landers' hospital!"

Charlie just shook his head.

"Is he going to be alright," J.B. inquired.

"Yeah. He is all taped up like a mummy. Reckon it will slow him down a while," Red replied. "Which reminds me. His dad, Thomas Blackfox, needs a job. Any chance of him getting on with the Bureau?"

"I could use him, helping to feed the horse herds, but I am about out of feed," Charlie answered. "Maybe you could get us some more money for hay."

"The brass seems to think that the big drive to thin out the herds would solve the grass shortage," J.B. added. "It was too late to help this winter, and it about cleaned out my budgeted funds!"

"I think that I can get the money. Send me some pictures of the stripped off grazing and some gaunt horses." Red stood up. "I want to get home before that storm blows in!"

"You might be starting too late." J.B. indicated his window view, which showed snowflakes beginning to fall. "Give me a call when you arrive."

Red nodded and began to button his coat. He was quickly out the door.

Red felt fortunate that the snow did not thicken. Although driving visibility was limited, and he was required to slow somewhat, he moved steadily towards Rawlins, apparently staying ahead of the main storm.

He placed a call to Irene, telling her that he would not see her that evening, as they had planned.

CHAPTER 31

Another Warning

Although it was still mid-afternoon, when Red arrived at his office, the cloud were so low and dark, it was like dusk. A week's mail was neatly stacked on his desk. A soiled envelope immediately aroused his curiosity!

It contained a single sheet of paper. On it, was a single sentence printed in large block letters, 'I WARNED YOU!!!'

Red stared at the note in amazement and then examined the envelope again. I contained neither stamp nor return address. Carrying the envelope, he went to the receptionist, whom he shared with Richard Cooper.

"Say, Gwen, do you remember getting this envelope?"

"Why, yes, Red. A little Indian boy dropped it off this afternoon. He said a white man paid him a dollar to bring it to me," Gwen frowned. "Is something wrong?"

"No. No, I was just curious, as it had no stamp." Red headed back to his office.

Back at his desk, Red ignored his other mail and sat staring at the block letters!

"Who warned me of what? Sounds like I didn't heed his warning! What am I supposed to do about it? If the aim is to make me sweat, it's done that! Have I teed someone off lately?"

Red suddenly leaned forward and pounded the desk with his fist!

"Stonewood! It has to be Stonewood! But why?"

Red got to his feet and paced around his small office for a few minutes.

"Stonewood must have heard of my promotion and figures I will kill all his business in Wyoming; which I will! Maybe Walt heard from him, too."

Red returned to his desk chair and dialed Walt's number.

"Hi, Walt. I just got back from Cody and there was a note delivered to my office. It just says 'I warned you'. Have you received any threats of any kind?"

"No. Nothing here, Red. You think it is Stonewood?"

"Can't think of anyone else, Walt. I figure he is upset with my promotion, and figures Wyoming is finished with his big drives. Which it is."

"What are you going to do, Red," Walt asked.

"I can't think of anything except pray,' Red replied. "I don't have a clue of, what he will do or, of course, even if it is Stonewood."

"Well, watch your back, pard!" Walt rang off.

The storm had passed through by Saturday noon so Red decided to drive on to Laramie to see Irene. He checked into a motel, as usual, and called her to announce his safe arrival.

An hour later, they were sitting in a quiet booth of his favorite restaurant, waiting for the arrival of their dinner. The faint odor of broiling steaks reached them.

"Honey, when are we going to get married," Red inquired, as he set down his wine glass.

"My college semester is over the first week of June." Irene blushed slightly. "Is that too soon?"

"I suppose. I will wait that long, if I have to." Red grimaced. "What about next year? You need another year to graduate, don't you?"

"I thought-, I hoped, we could find a little place near Elk Mountain," Irene said hesitantly. "It's about half way

186

between Laramie and Rawlins. It would be about a forty-five minute drive for each of us, until I get my degree." She finished with a rush. "Darling, you would't mind if I finished college, would you?"

"Well, gee, Honey. What about kids? You do want a family, don't you?" Red felt himself tense up slightly.

"Of course, I do, Darling, but couldn't we wait a year or two?" Irene's face was beet red at that point.

The salads arrived to interrupt their conversation. Red raised his hands in surrender.

"As long as we don't wait too long."

During dinner, Red told of his trip to Cody and about the Indian lad, Bucky.

"Oh, Red! He could have died of exposure, if you hadn't looked for him. The poor boy," Irene exclaimed.

"Well, he is going to be fine," Red responded. "And it didn't crush his spirit any."

They had finished dessert before Red decided to tell about the warning note. Irene' face was a picture of despair.

"It's Stonewood, isn't it?" It was a statement, not a question.

"I'm afraid so," Red admitted.

"Darling, what are you going to do?" There was a bit of panic in Irene's voice.

"All I can think of is to establish my program as quickly as possible, so there would be no point in threatening me," Red replied. "I have the Rock Springs area to set up, yet and I need to get the funds to feed some of the herds until spring. After that, the system should run itself."

The month of May brought a much needed rain, and warmer weather. Red was able to secure sufficient funds to keep the wild horses from starving. The teams, which he set up, capitalized on his experience and trapped many herds with the use of hay.

It had been several weeks, since he had received the warning note, and He began to feel that it was just a hoax.

That month also saw the marriage of Teresa to Walt Wiley. They were married in a small chapel in Laramie with a few close friends attending.

———

187

Walt's brother, Ben, was his best man and the two of them were clad in dark blue western cut suits with bolo ties. Walt's bolo contained a dollar sized Marine Corps emblem and Ben's a horse head. Teresa wore traditional white, but in an ankle length gown and matching white hat with a small veil. Irene, the bridesmaid wore a similar gown of pink. The bride carried a single red rose nestled in greenery.

The rose was tossed lightly to Irene under the small shower of rice at the end of the ceremony.

After the wedding, the couple set out for Phoenix in Teresa's jeep. Walt was to be provided with a State's vehicle, so left his pick-up with his sister, Beth. The newlyweds would honeymoon in a motel there, until they found a suitable apartment or house. Teresa would continue to write and submit her work from there.

CHAPTER 32

Kidnapped

Irene had set the date of their marriage to be June the twenty-first. It was Saturday night now, and they were dining at the same restaurant, as they had visited on their first date. As on their first date, Irene watched with amusement as Red attacked his rack of ribs.

With a sigh of contentment, Red finally wiped his hands and tossed down his napkin.

"I stopped in to see Bucky last week. They were supposed to take off the cast yesterday. They told him to stay off Smokey for at least two weeks after. He was pretty bummed. I think he expected everything to be returned to normal, when the cast came off."

"It must have been hard for him," Irene sympathized. "He was used to so much freedom."

"Probably was a good vacation for his Mother," Red laughed. "Charlie is real happy with his Dad's work ethics, too, so that is working out."

They chatted at their table for a half hour or so, before Red paid the check, and they strolled out. It was a warm sultry evening, as Red remarked, when they had reached his car.

"Three more weeks until the wedding. I wish it was tomorrow," Red remarked as he drove toward Irene's apartment.

"No, no! I'm not near ready," Irene protested.

Red rolled down the window as he parked the car in front of Irene's apartment house and shut off the ignition. He reached across the seat to draw her close for a goodnight kiss.

They were too engrossed in each other to notice the large black sedan that eased in behind them. Neither did they see the figures that emerged from the car and approached on either side of Red's vehicle.

Suddenly the beam from a small flashlight lit up the front seat of Red's car. It also revealed a black automatic pistol, trained directly on Red.

"Well, now, ain't this romantic," a rough voice simpered, and then quickly changed to a snarl. "Out of the car. Both of you. Quickly!"

"Who are you? What do you want," Red demanded.

"Shut up! Turn around and stick your hands behind you, or we'll rough up the girl," the voice answered angrily.

"Let her go. I'll do whatever you want," Red persisted.

Irene let out a small scream as the man, who pulled her out of the car, gave her arm a twist.

"We told you. Speak again and I'll break her arm," the second man barked.

Wisely, Red suppressed a reply and felt the cold steel of handcuffs closing around his wrists. Hands felt over his body, looking for a firearm.

Red was shoved into the front seat of the sedan.

"Handcuff her to the grab bar," the first voice instructed the second man. "And get those blindfolds out of the trunk."

In a matter of minutes, black hoods were dropped over Red and Irene's heads and the car pulled away from the curb. The driver made a series of turns, both right and left, designed to confuse the captive's directional sense.

When the big car straightened out and began to pick up speed, Red was unsure whether they were headed north or west. A few long curves contributed to his complete loss of direction.

There was little or no conversation between the two captors, leading Red to believe, they were not well

---

acquainted: certainly not friends. Red was afraid to ask questions lest they fulfil their threat to harm Irene. He dare not try to comfort her.

The miles sped by. The steady drone of the car engine tended to lull Red to sleep in spite of the seriousness of their situation. It had been a long day plus the two-hour drive from Rawlins, and his was tired. Twice, they pulled over to the side of the road to change drivers. The second time, one of them went to the trunk and pulled out some heavy objects. Red smelled gasoline. They were replenishing the fuel tank.

"We must have come at least two hundred miles, probably two fifty. That would take us to Rock Springs area, if we went straight west, or Landers to the northwest, or Buffalo is to the north. I give up. I'm not sure that we didn't go east into Colorado! Guess I'll know eventually."

Convinced that he would probably need his strength, Red no longer fought to stay awake, but drifted off to sleep.

Red was awakened by the car driving onto the shoulder and stopping. This time, there was some conversation between the two abductors.

"We're down below a quarter tank. I think we should put the rest of the gas in," one of them said. "I don't like full cans of gas rolling around in the trunk on a rough road, anyhow."

"The GPS says it is fifteen more miles to the turn-off," the other replied. "Might as well get it done with now."

There was more noise from the trunk and again, the odor of gasoline drifted into the car.

Back on the road, Red began to smell pine forests. Shortly, the car slowed to make a hard left turn; the crunch of tires on gravel indicated that they had left the main road.

The smell of the forest was strong now, and the car move slower, swinging back and forth as the driver dodged potholes. Unable to hang onto anything, Red was flung around in the seat. His captors had not taken the trouble to fasten his safety belt. The driver cursed, as the car bounced into and out of holes, he was unable to avoid.

After what seemed to be an eternity, the driver braked to a stop and cut the engine. The men wasted no time in jerking them out of the car.

"Where the hell have you been? You should have been here hours ago." Red recognized the voice to be that of Rick Stonewood.

"We couldn't pick them up earlier, cuz they had people around them, Mister Stonewood. We had to wait till they ate and came back to the apartment.

"Did anybody see you?"

"No, Sir. No one."

"Hello, Stonewood. Fancy meeting you here." Red's voice was muffled by the hood.

"Take off those hoods." Stonewood ignored Red's greeting. "Lock them in the back bedroom, Rufe." He instructed the man, who stood beside him.

Red's quick eyes took in his surroundings as he was hustled through the house. The place was more palatial, than would be expected for the middle of the woods. The floors were tiled with expensive throw rugs, and a glimpse of the kitchen indicated all modern appliances.

As the bedroom door shut, they heard the key turn in the lock. Irene had been released from the cufflinks at the car. She rushed over to Red and held him close, her eyes were wide and her face was ashen.

"Red, I'm so frightened. What are they going to do to us?"

"I don't know, Darling. We have to be brave and pray to God for His protection." Red kissed her forehead.

Red edged over to the window with Irene still clinging to him and was amazed to find an Olympic sized swimming pool in the back yard. It was surrounded by a large concrete patio, with a number of umbrella covered tables and plastic tubular lounge chairs. This place was built for parties!

Tree covered hills were all around them. He could just make out the dirt road that led to the house, off to the left. To the right, a far distant snowcapped mountain shone in the early afternoon sun. Birds were busy flitting from one tree to another. It was a serene and lovely sight, in contrast to the fear and anxiety in the hearts of the onlookers!

The so-called bedroom was more like a family room, although a large king-sized bed graced one corner of the room. Red led Irene to a large sofa. Behind it was a wall-covered bookcase, filled with books, many of them untouched in their dust covers.

Irene began to recover from her terror with a faint color reappearing in her face. Red laid his head on her shoulder as he pleaded with His Heavenly Father for protection. She kissed him, as he finished and echoed his "Amen".

They heard the key turn in the door lock and both turned that direction with apprehension spreading across their faces.

Rufe entered, pushing a cart with covered dishes upon it. The aroma of hot food emanating from it was overpowering, as it had been many hours since their restaurant dinner. Rufe said nothing, but motioned for Red to turn his back, while he unlocked his handcuffs. He then retreated to the door, and let himself out. The key turned in the lock.

"Lord, bless this meal," Red announced as he advanced and whipped off the cloth. A savory sight of meat, potatoes and vegetables greeted his eyes. Two mugs of steaming coffee completed the repast before him.

"Oh, I couldn't eat anything," Irene demurred.

"But you must," Red insisted. "You need to keep up your strength for what lies ahead. I may need you to assist me, or at least to keep up. If we can hold out until tomorrow afternoon, we have a chance."

Hope flooded Irene's face. "Red, you have a plan?"

"Yes, but don't press me. It's all off if they suspect anything. Now come and eat." Red handed her a plate of food and a mug of coffee.

Irene discovered more of an appetite than she thought and managed to eat most of her food. Red had no problem with his and finished hers, too.

Rick Stonewood did not keep them in suspense long, but unlocked the door and entered shortly after they had finished eating.

CHAPTER 33

Forest Fire

Red did not wait for Stonewood to voice his complaint, but attacked immediately.

"I can't believe, Rick Stonewood that you are so petty and stupid to think my promotion will ruin your business to a point, where you will risk murder. You must know that another man will take my place and the day of the big drives are over."

Stonewood stared at Red in amazement!

"You think you are here because of your stinking promotion? I don't give a s--t for your stinking promotion. They can make you a General of the Army for all I care. I am going to kill you for ratting on me to my son!"

It was Red's turn to gape in surprise!

"You can't be serious! I never spoke to George about you. Not once."

"I don't believe you. George left me a long message on the phone. He mentioned you and knew all about my reputation. He wants to meet me and save me from my sin. You, bastard, you told him everything." Stonewood's face was contorted with pain and anger. He turned toward the door.

"Wait, Rick, you've got it all wrong." Red sprang toward him, but Stonewood was out the door. The lock clicked behind him.

Rick Stonewood strode into the family room where his hired help was sitting.

Rufe, load up. We are going back to Phoenix. You two, take them to a ravine up in the hills and knock them off. Conceal the bodies the best you can and check in with me in my office."

"Boss," Rufe spoke up. "Have you been listening to the thunder? There is a storm brewing in the hills." He pointed out the window. "Looks like a fire started, probably from lightning."

Stonewood took one look out the window and turned to Rufe. "Let's go now! I don't want to be caught in this God forsaken place." He rushed for the big SUV parked in the front yard

Rufe followed him, carrying a couple of small suitcases. Quickly tossing them in the back, he climbed into the driver's seat and backed out. As they drove, the smell of smoke grew prevalent.

"Boss, I don't think this is a good idea. It looks like we are driving right into the fire area," Rufe complained.

"Shut up and keep driving. There is no other way out. We'll just close the vents and drive right through it," Stonewood snarled, fear creeping into his voice.

Ash was drifting down on the vehicle now and the smell of smoke was strong. Stonewood reached over and turned the air conditioner to "on" and "inside air".

"Damn lumberjacks don't know how to build a road," Rick growled as the car hit a deep pothole. "Can't you drive faster?"

Rufe was too busy driving to answer. The waves of smoke were heavy and the visibility was down to only a few hundred feet and dropping.

"Boss, this is crazy! We got to turn back." Rufe's voice went up an octave and his knuckles were white on the steering wheel.

"No! We got to get out of here," Stonewood insisted. "We can make it."

Flames could be seen through the smoke. The air conditioner was making little headway against the heat from outside. Both men were sweating profusely.

A wind gust momentarily blew the smoke from in front of them, revealing a wall of flames from the ground to well above the treetops.

"Stop! Turn around," Stonewood shrieked in terror, but Rufe had already stomped on the brakes.

He backed swiftly into a u-turn, his back wheels dropping into the shallow ditch. The wheels spun briefly, then took hold and the car sprang ahead. Paint was flaking off the exterior as the car retreated. A burning limb crashed down ahead of them, but the heavy SUV blasted over it and kept going! The fire seemed to keeping pace with them as Rufe's progress was slowed by the lack of visibility and the condition of the road.

Finally, the smoke thinned to the point where they could speed up, and they rapidly pulled ahead into clear air. Neither spoke, as they retraced their route back the house. The fact that Stonewood's stubbornness had almost gotten them both roasted, was not brought up.

Back at the house, things were not going smoothly either. Both Red and Irene had been handcuffed with their hands behind their backs and taken from their room. Frank, the older one, wanted to hustle their captives into the hills and dispose of them, as they had been instructed. Lang, the younger, wanted to "have some fun" with the good-looking female before killing them.

Irene was shaking in terror, more at the thought of being sexually attacked, than being murdered. Red was livid with rage with his inability to come to her aid.

"Even if I was inclined to allow you to abuse this poor girl, Lang, look outside at that smoke. It's a lot closer than it was. We don't have time to waste," Frank argued.

"Aw, don't be such an old lady. You go ahead with the redhead and a shovel. I'll be along, before he gets a hole dug." Lang strode over to Irene and reached for the neck of her blouse as she shrank away from him.

"Oh, please," Irene turned imploring eyes on Frank. "Don't let him touch me!"

"Aw, come on, Darlin. A little lovin never hurt

anyone," Lang again reached for her blouse.

"Stop it, Lang." The tone of Frank's voice gave Lang a pause. He glanced at his partner.

Frank was holding his black automatic pistol at eye level, pointed directly at Lang's head.

"You touch that girl, and I will plant you in the hole with them." Frank's cold level voice left no doubt of his sincerity.

"Frank! You can't be ser--."

"Shut up and take your pistol out of your shoulder holster. Carefully! Now, toss it on the couch. That a boy. The knife at your ankle. Make it join your pistol. Now, stretch out face down in the middle of the rug." Frank dug into his pocket with his left hand and withdrew a ring of keys.

He motioned Irene to come over to him and turn her back. He unlocked her handcuffs.

"I'm going to let you go, but you need me to get you out of here," he told her. "There is a wood shed to the left out the front door. Go get me two spades from there."

"Oh, please. Let Red go. He didn't do what Mister Stonewood thinks he did," Irene begged.

"Sorry, can't do that," Frank said abruptly. "Now move. Go get those shovels."

"Do as he says, Honey. He is sticking out his neck enough as it is," Red interposed. "Frank, I am eternally grateful to you for sparing her."

Reluctantly, Irene moved to open the door. She let out a little scream!

"They are coming back! Mister Stonewood is coming back."

They heard the SUV pull up to the house and stop. Frank thought fast.

"Get up, Lang and get your gun back. We'll forget about back there. He'll kill you for attacking the girl and kill me for turning her loose. Girl, get over here next to your man. Everybody keep your mouths shut."

Rick Stonewood burst through the door.

"We're all going to be burnt up! That forest fire is coming this way like a locomotive. There ain't no way out."

197

"You mean there isn't a trail or anything we can drive out on?" Frank stared at him in disbelief.

"Nope. I remember, the agent laughing, when he gave me the keys. He said 'don't get caught in there, there's only one way out'." Rick slumped into a chair, despair written all over him.

"I know how to save us." All heads swiveled toward Red.

"What do you mean? How are you going to do that?" Stonewood's face showed a glimmer of hope.

"I didn't say that I was going to. I said I know how." Red grinned.

"Come on, man. Tell us," Lang implored.

"Now why would I do that? You would just kill Irene and me and save yourselves." Red's grin became almost a sneer.

Rick Stonewood leaped to his feet. His eyes radiating new life.

"I promise you, no one will harm you. You know me. I keep my word," he panted. "You're getting married. I'll give you a hundred thousand wedding gift! Please!"

Red's grin vanished. "Yes, I've heard that you do keep your word. I'll do it. Get these cuffs off me."

At a nod from his boss, Frank moved over to Red and in seconds, Red was free!

"I need some insurance from your hired apes. I want Lang's gun," Red directed.

Lang started to protest, but was silenced by a scowl from Stonewood. He reluctantly laid his automatic on the table.

"Now your knife and sheathe," Red added.

With the armaments in his possession, Red became all business.

"Frank, go the woodshed and bring out what saws that are there. We will be in the back yard. Rick, drag several blankets off the beds. Honey, you stay here by the door and watch the fire. When you see flames, join us in the back. You other two, come with me."

Red and the other two trotted out into the back yard. Red threw the cushions off the nearest chaise lounge as Frank

---

ran up, carrying an old carpenter saw and two log saws. Red grabbed one of them and showed Rufe, where he wanted him to cut the chair up.

"Frank, do the same on another one. Lang, help him hold it, while he saws."

By the time Rick appeared with his armload of blankets, Red had two cane-shaped pipes cut from the plastic lounge chair. Two to three feet long, they would be the breathing tubes for them as they stood or sat in the swimming pool, as the fire raged above them.

"Throw them in the shallow end of the pool and weight them down with some rocks," Red instructed Rick. "We might need them to put out fires, afterward and covers from the cold later."

The smell of smoke was strong now, and ashes began to drift over them. Seven tubes of varying length lay on the hard packed dirt pool deck now, and Irene rushed out of the house.

"Red, the fire is huge. How are you going to save us from that?"

"Okay, you all. Here is what you do. Each of you grab a tube. We are going to all get in the pool and stay below the surface using these tubes to breathe through until the fire goes by."

"I can't swim," wailed Lang. "I'll drown."

"No, you won't, stupid. You just sit on your fat butt in the shallow end and suck air through the tube," Frank responded.

"That's it. Pick out a breathing tub of your choice and be sure to keep your lips tight around the pipe or water will leak in. The house will undoubtable burn, so we may have to stay under for a good while." Red was finished with his instructions. "Now I am going to pray to my Heavenly Father for deliverance. You may join me or not!"

"Lord, I know most of us aren't worthy of Your Grace, but I ask You to save us from this fire storm, anyhow. Amen."

Hot embers began to fall around them, hissing as they hit the pool surface. Red waved them toward the pool and with Irene cling tightly to an arm, he jumped in feet first into the water.

With the gale, created by the fire, sending flaming embers ahead of the flames, the trees surrounding the house were soon burning. The woodshed, being the closest to the trees, was the first to ignite. Pine logs, stacked inside, contributed to a furnace like atmosphere and the intensity of the heat soon lit off the main house.

Cedar shake shingles and cedar siding, while pleasing to the eye, were poor choices in a forest fire condition. The house was soon totally engulfed in flames. The two vehicles were the last to join the inferno. The exploding gasoline tanks was felt by the inhabitants of the swimming pool. Numerous animals, fleeing ahead of the fire, also found refuge in the pool!

As the firestorm moved on down the valley and the foliage, which was, stripped from the trees by the flames, burned out, the flames and heat began to wane. Red was watching the progress of the fire, through several inches of water. Finally, he moved to the far side of the pool and ventured a quick peek above the water. The heat from the still burning house beat down on him like a club and he quickly ducked back under.

"Another half hour, maybe," he muttered to himself.

Slowly the flames died down in the house, as everything flammable had been consumed. Red again raised head from the water, this time the air was hot, but livable, and he climbed from the pool. The others, feeling the disturbance of the water slowly followed him. They were a waterlogged crew!

"Each of you grab a blanket; it will be your bed tonight, and be careful where you step," Red directed. "It will be sundown soon. Frank, you and Lang, find some burning stumps to drag over to the road. We may need some heat with all these wet clothes in the cool night air."

"I hear a couple of planes," Rufe offered. "Probably the fire fighters. Maybe one will fly over and check out the house."

"I think it is best to hang around here through tomorrow," Red agreed. "Someone will be by sooner or later."

As the light faded, the bedraggled group huddled around a credible campfire made from logs and branches that the men had gathered. All were coughing from the smoke tainted air. Their clothes had dried somewhat, but were still damp and cold. Red and Irene had an advantage in that they shared their blankets and body heat. The others were too macho to stoop to that, each shivering under their separate wet blanket.

Red faced Rick across the fire. "Rick, you wouldn't listen to me before, but you are going to have to now. I swear, I didn't breathe a word about you to your son."

"Don't give me that, Iverson. You are the only one that could have ratted on me," Rick insisted.

"That's not so, Rick. Anyone with a computer on the internet could find out your life story, any arrests and/or jail time, in a matter of days," Red responded. "Ask any of your men that use computers."

"He's right, Boss." Lang contributed. "It would be a piece of cake."

"But he didn't even know my name." Rick wasn't convinced.

"No, but a background check on his mother would turn up her marriage license, which would have your name on it, and it would be downhill from there," Red responded.

Rick surrendered. "What do I do now?"

"Well, if you are asking my advice, I would suggest you find a new business, one that you don't have to scare off your competition. Meet with George, apologize for your past, and mean it," Red answered. "Dropping a couple hundred thousand of your ill-gotten gains on his mother, to make up for all the child support that you didn't pay, might help."

Probably, being scared out of his wits in the car, total despair after escaping the firestorm and his sudden salvation in the swimming pool had taken its toll on Rick Stonewood. He was a chastened, humbled man!

"I'll do it! Maybe the God, who you worship is for real, after all. I'll close up Drover's Inc. I don't know, what I can do after that. I don't know anything except driving horses."

201

Red had a sudden inspiration! "I know just the business, Rick. You have most of the equipment and the pilots. Trade out your little helicopters for some big tank carriers and go into the contract forest fire fighting business."

The dim firelight hid the surprise in Rick's face, but it was reflected in his voice. "Firefighting? Maybe I could! What's to know about it? You just fly over and drop some dust on the fire, and it goes out! My pilots can do that." The old arrogant, optimistic, Rick Stonewood was reappearing.

"It's been a long day and promises to be a long uncomfortable night, but I suggest that we get as much rest as we can," Red proposed. "I am going to give thanks to my Father for bringing us through the fire storm without injury. You all can join me or not!"

"Lord, we thank You for your deliverance from the fire, and for the inspiration, You gave me. We are still a long way from our homes with no transportation or food to get us there, and we thank You in advance, for what You are sending to us. Your will be done. Amen!" It was significant that Rick bowed his head for the prayer.

CHAPTER 34

Rescued

Red awoke with the sounds of one of the men adding fuel to the campfire. It was still dark and Red had no idea ,what time it was. The air was cool, but his clothes and blankets were only damp now, and Irene and he were warm, but stiff, from the discomfort of laying on the dirt. Some of the trees were burning like torches and, combined with the smoke, an eerie atmosphere surrounded them. He heard the sounds of helicopters and a light plane in the distance. With difficulty, he drifted back to a fitful sleep.

Dawn was breaking, when Red became aware of activity around him. Men were throwing off their blankets and standing up. One, Frank was stirring around the burned out remains of the house. Rufe joined him. He located a couple ceramic bowls, which he picked up.

"Rick, where did we get our drinking water from," Red inquired. His mouth dry and raw from the smoke.

"There was a pump and generator in the wood shed," was the response.

Red shook his head. "Frank, fill up one of those bowls with water from the pool. It won't be great, but it will be wet."

Frank arrived with a large cooking bowl filled with water. Rufe brought a second empty bowl. The water was covered with ashes and half-burnt debris that had blown in.

With the knife, which he had taken from Lang, Red slit the left arm of his shirt and tore it off at the elbow. Using it as a filter, he placed it over the empty bowl and held the edges, while Frank poured the dirty pool water into it. The result was a milky looking liquid that smelled of chlorine.

"Best I can do, Honey," he remarked as he offered the water to Irene. She made a face, as she bent to drink, but after a tentative sip, she drank thirstily and smiled her appreciation to Red and Frank.

This was repeated several times, until all had their fill.

The sun rose warm and bright, soon to complete drying the clothes. Rufe joined Lang in searching among the ashes of the house. Anything capable of being used as a chair was brought out, as all the logs around the clearing was either still burning or burned up.

Frank wondered aimlessly around for a bit, and then turned to Rick.

"Boss, don't think, it is much use, but I'm going to see if I can shoot something to eat. Maybe some rabbits hid in their burrow, until the fire past."

"Go ahead, Frank. Good luck," was Rick's response.

Red watched Frank draw his pistol. This reminded him of Lang's automatic, which he still had.

"Wonder if it still works after those hours in the pool and wet all night," he mentioned to Irene and drew the pistol from its shoulder holster.

The automatic was in surprising good shape. Lang had kept it well oiled, so only a trace of rust showed. Red released the magazine that held the bullets and thumbed out the bullets. Wiping each bullet dry with his remaining shirtsleeve, he laid them in a row beside him. He dry fired the now empty gun, satisfied that it was working correctly.

Lang heard the clicks from the empty gun and started walking over to see, what was causing them. Red noticed his approach and quickly slipped a couple of the dried cartridges into the magazine. He then inserted the magazine into the pistol and worked the slide to load the gun. The rest of the cartridges, he placed into his pocket. As he stood up, he heard the sounds of helicopters approaching. He looked up, but saw nothing.

Lang held out a hand as he approached.

"I want my gun back," he snarled.

"Not a chance," Red replied. He still held the pistol in his right hand.

"Then I'll take it," Lang gritted out as he leaped at Red, grabbing at his pistol arm. At the same time, he jammed his elbow into Red's ribs.

Red fell over backward, but aimed a knee at Lang's groin. Red's arm struck the ground with considerable force and the gun skidded across the short distance to where Rick was sitting. Rick picked up the weapon and let the hammer down to a safety position, but kept it ready.

The sound of the helicopters was loud, now, but neither of the combatants noticed, as they grappled in the dirt.

Suddenly two helicopter burst into view and dropped down onto the road. The word "Police" stencilled across their sides. Three men jumped out of the first one with guns drawn and leveled at Rick.

"Put the gun down, now," cried the foremost police officer. Rick complied instantly!

The other two ran to Irene's side.

"Are you Miss Fallon, and are you all right?"

"Yes, to both questions," Irene replied.

"Which one of these is Red Iverson," was the next question.

Before Irene could answer, a fourth man approached from the second helicopter. Irene recognized him to be Richard Cooper, Red's ex-boss.

"Irene, are you okay? Where is Red?"

Wordlessly, Irene pointed to the two fighters who were scrambling to their feet. She then threw her arms around Richard.

"Praise the Lord! I'm so happy to see you!"

"Richard patted her shoulder and looked over to where the police were handcuffing the three men.

"Don't cuff the ugly redhead. He's the one we are looking for," he announced.

Red hurried over, his mouth stretched in a broad grin.

He received an unprecedented hug from his ex-boss.

"Glad to see you, Red. We were concerned, when the bug went dead yesterday. We were afraid that it had been discovered. Decided to come to the last known spot."

"That was, when we went for a four hour swim to escape the fire. I was afraid, it wouldn't survive the soaking, but had no choice," Red explained

Red pulled off his left boot and gave the heel a half turn. It came off in his hand, revealing a hollow spot in the middle. Red shook out a tiny electronic homing device.

"We went into a swimming pool in the back yard to escape the flames," Red explained. "I didn't think it would survive."

The senior police officer walked over to join them.

"If you have the missing man, Director. I would like to take everybody back to the station and sort it all out there."

At Richard Cooper's approval, Rick, Lang and Rufe were escorted to the first helicopter, all in handcuffs and the others went with the senior police officer to the second. Red, remembering Frank's assistance in protecting Irene, elected to remain silent regarding the missing fourth man. He would have to find his own way back. He did reveal this information to the senior police officer on the way back to Rawlins.

CHAPTER 35

George Finds Out

The helicopter carrying Red touched down briefly in front of the Rawlins police station and let him and his party out. It then continued on to Cheyenne. Rick and his thugs would be tentatively charged there with kidnapping and attempted murder.

Red and Irene were taken to a conference room and asked by Detective Payne, the detective in charge, to write a transcript of their experience. He read the transcripts carefully, when they had finished and leaned back in his chair.

"So neither of you actually seen you captors, prior to being released from the car," he asked.

"No, Detective Payne, we did not." Red answered for both of them.

"Just call me Irwin. So it could have been any of the four men that you saw at the cabin, the detective responded.

"No. I have spoken to Rick Stonewood many times," Red stated. "I would have recognized his voice. Also, Rufe was his driver, so that leaves Lang and Frank as our captors."

"That is a logical deduction, but a clever lawyer could twist it until a jury could doubt the facts. I'll see what the District Attorney has to say." Irwin Payne stood up. "I guess Mister Cooper will get you to your homes."

207

It was close to midnight when Red wearily crawled into bed. One of Mister Cooper's staff had driven Red and Irene back to Laramie, where Red picked up his car. Ruefully, he removed a parking ticket from his windshield and drove back to Rawlins.

It had been a long and tiring day, but he was too tightly wound to go immediately to sleep. His mind drifted back over the events of the last two days.

"Would I really want Rick Stonewood locked up for several years," he wondered to himself.

Detective Payne had seemed doubtful of a conviction of abduction, and no chance at all for attempted murder. Not actual attempt to harm them had taken place.

Parting with Irene had been tearful, as she was afraid to be alone at night. He had suggested an early marriage and she had wavered.

That would solve some problems!

How about George Harris, Rick's son? His father's record was bad enough without a prison record!

It was almost three o'clock, when Red last looked at his watch. He finally slept.

It took several cups of coffee to charge Red's system. Even so, he arrived late at his office. On his desk was a memo from Richard Cooper:

Stonewood, Lang and Rufe were released after a substantial bond was posted. The District Attorney wants you to call him after one P.M.

There was also a note to call Walt Wiley, when he had time. Red was reaching for the office phone, when his cell phone chirped.

"Red, this is George Harris. I just learned that Rick Stonewood, my- uh, my father has been arrested for kidnapping and attempted murder." George's voice sounded anguished. "Your and Miss Fallon's names were mentioned."

"I'm so sorry, George. I tried to discourage you from looking for your father. I'm really sorry you found him," Red responded sincerely.

"You knew about him all along. We didn't just meet by accident, did we?" George's voice was slightly accusing.

"No George, it wasn't by accident. Your fa--, Rick Stonewood was threatening me, and some of my friends. I had a wild idea about using you as a club over his head to stop him. It was a bad idea and I did abandon the idea. But before I came to my senses, I revealed to him that I had met you," Red admitted. "Your father isn't a bad man at heart; he just makes some bad decisions!"

"The murder and kidnapping charge, what was that all about? Is he that bad?"

"Well, it was kind of a misunderstanding. Rick Stonewood was quite serious, about your not locating him, and when you contacted him, he assumed that I had let the cat out of the bag." Red was reluctant to go further.

"So, did he have you kidnapped?" George probed.

"Yes. That's what it is called."

"Damn it, Red. Talk to me." George was losing patience.

"All right, George. He had us kidnapped and hauled to a cabin in the woods! When a forest fire threatened, he told his hired thugs to kill us and hide our bodies in the woods. I had a GPS bug in my boot and the cops rescued us. That's the bones of it," Red blurted out.

"You mean, he was going to have you killed for telling me about him?" George's voice was a mixture of incredibility and anguish.

"I'm sorry you had to hear this, George."

"What can I do, Red," George pleaded.

"I wish I had a good answer, George. Keep praying for him and keep trying to make contact with him," Red replied. "He had a scare, up in the hills: maybe he will change."

"Thanks, Red. You've been a good friend." Red could feel his friend's despondence.

After putting away his cell phone, Red picked up the office phone and asked his receptionist to get the District Attorney on the phone.

The District Attorney wasted no time or words before getting to the point.

"I read you transcripts. At any time, did you feel that your life was in immediate danger? Was any effort to offer you or the lady any physical harm, other than that sexual move on her?"

"No, Sir." Red replied. "Only when Stonewood instructed them to take us out in the woods and bury the bodies."

"But that could be construed by an outsider to be only scare tactics, couldn't it?"

"Yes, I reckon it could," Red answered, doubtfully.

"I'm sorry, Iverson. There is no way that we can prove attempted murder. Moreover, with no positive identification on which of the men actually performed the abduction, I can only charge them all with false imprisonment. With the forest fire complicating the picture, I might not make that stick, either, but I am willing to try."

Red barely restrained himself from swearing, as he hung up the phone!

Epilogue

Red and Irene were married in a small ceremony at Jana Lake, where they first met, with her father doing the honors. They spent a good part of their honeymoon in the desert on horseback, among the wild horse herds.

Irene was able to complete her college studies before giving birth to a baby girl. The little baby, named June, inherited her mother's beauty and her father's red hair and gentle disposition.

They bought a small house on ten acres on the outskirts of Rawlins and kept a couple of riding horses.

The trial of Stonewood and associates held little surprises, in that they were convicted of false imprisonment. Lang received the longest sentence, probably due to his past record of violence. Strangely enough, Rick Stonewood received a comparatively short sentence: shortened further by good behavior.

Rick came out of prison a changed man; however and eventually established a relationship with his son, George Harris. As of this writing, George was still praying for his father's conversion into Christianity.

Frank was never seen or heard of again. Whether he died in the woods, or walked out to begin a new life, is not known.

The Wyoming wild horse herds became renowned for their grace and beauty. Red instigated an annual horse auction that brought buyers from all over the continent. Owning a Wyoming wild horse became an "in" thing among horses lovers.

Under Walt's direction, Arizona also improved its wild horse herds. The two states would swap studs to control inbreeding.

The Old West traditions live on through its wild horse hunters. May the wild herds continue to roam free in the forests and deserts of the West.